Summer Point

Summer Point

LINDA McNUTT

CORMORANT
BOOKS

The publisher gratefully acknowledges the support
of the Canada Council, the Ontario Arts Council, and the
Canadian Department of Heritage.

Edited by Gena K. Gorrell.
Cover design by Bill Douglas@The Bang,
with Janice Wright Cheney's mixed media and collage on
paper, *Vera*, (1994) from her Women in Fiction series.
Author photo by G.R. McNutt.

Printed and bound in Canada.

Cormorant Books Inc.
RR 1
Dunvegan, Ontario
Canada K0C 1J0

Canadian Cataloguing in Publication Data
McNutt, Linda, 1966-
Summer point
ISBN 1-896951-01-5
I. Title.
PS8576.C498S85 1997   C813'.54   C97-900229-X
PR9199.3.M3365S85 1997

With thanks to
Bob, Bobbie, Kevin, John, Joan
and the cottages at the Point.

I Arrivals

Title

I shaped the red clay cranes again last night. We used to watch them dissolving in the cold salt rain. They stained everything they touched. Blood and clean red earth. Shore colours, the colours of the shore world here in autumn.

James is inside sleeping the morning through. We are back at the shore. Back, I guess, only for me. He has not been brought here before. The shore. My shore. Recent inheritance. I called my father first and told him that his sister had decided. I will be given title — not Dad, not my brother, not anyone who could lift the shutters or carry the pump back to the car in the fall. Not anyone who could run the gas-powered lawnmower, not anyone who could fix the stovepipe, not anyone competent. Me. Aunt Maud has broken another tradition.

Duenna, she said implying a future, and now I inherit....

I spent this morning picking away at the bones of the old cottage. My family cottage has always stood at Indian Point. It is a white-washed constant in the salt wind that twists in off the Northumberland Strait. In this last weekend of summer I am in charge, for the first time, of closing the cottage.

It is a place in the world that is shuttered against the locals every fall and opened for the summer people every spring. No one was ever explicit about what the locals might do over the winter, but The Aunts whispered of beer bottles, and we all hate the thought of fire.

None of this is discussed.

In the cottage generation of my family, the rocking chair women who understood the complexities of second cousins once removed and knew the names of sister-in-laws step-children's husbands, and how to drop stitches in their knitting, very little is discussed. They pretended that the world could be organized.

The fall, though, is beyond our efforts. It is the season of electrifying wind. Its storms wash parts of the world up here every year. Pipes, salt-worn pieces of glass and pottery, broken lobster traps in from the bay, and people. I have found myself washed up onto this shore at various times. Mostly, like now, when I need the ghosts.

While James sleeps the morning out, I am making lists. Lists of what has been done and what will need to happen before the ice comes in. Winter preparation. Here decisions are real. They have meaning and place and references in memory. So I am making lists the way my Aunt Maud used to. Lists of real, lasting and important things to do. Aunt Maud's sweater is smaller since last year. I wear it against the breeze, but my feet are warm on the veranda boards.

Aunt Maud said she knew less every year she made them.

My family has been pulled back into history now, the part of it that summered here is gone, but every board and stone, and the sound of the jangling cottage keys in my hand, brings strong unsorted moments back. Nothing ever keeps its ordered place.

My Aunt Maud said I too would know less every year. She was right.

The Leapings of Wind

Whenever we went to the shore as a family, we had to do "the visiting" first. Even if we had only a weekend there to immerse ourselves, we were forced to visit. Wasting precious seconds we might need to transform ourselves into summer people. "Waving the family flag," my father called it. "Close your eyes and think of England," he'd say to my mother, and she'd wrinkle up her face.

This visiting was with The Aunts. Unlike my Aunt Maud, these Aunts were great-aunts, my grandmother's living sisters, but we called them aunts to avoid confusion and to imply a closeness that pleased my grandmother. They lived in a big white house in town across the field from their brother's leaning, shingled house. Their brother, our Uncle K, abbreviated to the initial sixty years earlier by The Aunts to keep him straight, in conversation, from their father, Kendal, mowed the twisting path that ran between the houses once a week. I told my brother the path was kept so Uncle K could bring them food. I told him that The Aunts had always lived in the sunporch. It was easy for him to believe, as they were always there when he visited. They sat and watched the traffic not go by, with the heaters running even in the heat of July. It was the one place in the village that the wind could not get into.

My brother and I were required to sit, with our hair combed, drinking tea for fifteen minutes. It doesn't seem such an ordeal now, but then it was torture.

Aunt Byrd had been married to the local government in the person of my Uncle Edward. It was considered a disgrace to die young in my family unless you had earned it. He had earned it; Uncle Edward had been in Parliament. Uncle Edward had owned the woollen mill and got the blanket contracts from the CNR. He had bought the organ for the Presbyterian church, and it had held its tune through all the thousand Sundays my Aunt Byrd played it.

My Aunt Wynd was less lucky in affairs of the heart, and of the village. She was also the moving one of the two. She hovered. She never sat down to eat, but nibbled out of saucers like an insecure and wary cat. She had been jilted at the altar. Later, she had married badly. Disgrace stretched into her life even after her husband departed his own, because his daughters came up from Boston and took "everything". Aunt Wynd was subtly at fault for not having raised these adult stepchildren to respect our family better.

"Taking everything" was what other people's sly and badly brought-up relatives did. They arrived at deaths and went to the lawyers' offices before the funerals. That was where they got "everything". I assumed that this meant the body. I couldn't figure out what else you wanted from a dead person. I had visions of bloodthirsty relatives descending on cooling bodies before anyone else had the chance. They got "everything".

What this actually meant should have been clear to us. The Aunts would tell us to be nice to them. The Aunts might leave us something special if we were good.

I hoped it would be a vital organ in a jar.

They had someone's metal replacement hip in a jar upstairs. I showed it to my brother and told him it was a real hip. I told him Aunt Wynd never sat still because she had only one hip and that affected her balance. He believed it for a while. He believed most things I told him about the shore because I had gone there first. As he got to be older and more important, I reminded him more often of my position as first-born and first-there. I had first rights to the hip. We both wanted to read the will at the lawyer's office when the time came. We did not yet associate inheritance with death; we just wanted to get something.

I hoped we would not get anything in the sunporch.

§

The voices scratched the surface of the air in the porch. A huge black fly buzzed stupidly into death between the panes of glass. Three inches above it, the glass parted from the screen. It would not move, though. It buzzed slowly and lazily to death in the sun-thick air.

I watched my brother try to set it free. He looked around and then casually reached out to kick the screen. The sound was ignored, but ignored malevolently. When everyone in the room had lost the exact pitch of his kick against the aluminum, conversation shifted back into the air.

If I had done this in The Aunts' house I would have been sent outside, but they did not feel the need to rein in boys as tightly. I felt that my brother could stand on the table between The Aunts' chairs and pee his name onto the windows with impunity. He often says now that he envied me the assumption of ineptitude that follows girls around in a house like that. "I would always be told what to do," he said. "It provided guidance boys didn't get. It provided rules to break."

Each of us thought the other was the favourite until we were old enough to talk about our family impressions.

He did not spell out his name in golden letters, but every time he could he reached out to kick the door. It was the only movement in the sunporch air.

The milky tea in the thin china cups was the

only coolness around us. We still had shoes on. Our car legs had been extended only as far as the sunporch would allow.

Finally my mother whispered to my father. She whispered his name beneath the hearing of The Aunts. This was easy enough to do, as they were deaf, although they did not accept their loss of hearing. "Everyone mumbles these days," they said. "Elocution is not taught in schools. Nothing of any worth is now taught in the schools."

My mother was a teacher.

Finally, my mother whispered my father's name again. Then she stood up and looked at us. "We have got to get these children to the shore." She said it as if we had been whining for days. As if we were what The Aunts called "discipline problems". She said it as if she and my father would love to sit in the stilted air with The Aunts, swilling stove-boiled tea, all afternoon, and the only thing stopping her was the children. Us. She sighed resignedly and told us we'd better get ready to go. Did we have to use the washroom? None of this bladder-prying occurred at home.

My father also sighed and bent to kiss the faces of The Aunts. He too was resigned to his modern children. His sigh was long and soft and wistful, signifying his dismay at our impatient natures. It went against all our efforts to sit still and be good, but we didn't care. We recognized artistry when we heard it and had no objection to this efficient, time-saving, glorious betrayal.

We slunk behind my father to kiss The Aunts

and then followed him to the car. We crept into the back seat and waited for my mother to leave the door of the sunporch. She stood there talking to The Aunts and then reluctantly, remembering her burdens, she drew herself away and into the car. She folded herself in beside my father and waved sadly all the way out of the yard and down the streets of town.

By the time we reached the shore, the salt grasses were twisted through the scents of the car. My father's tie disappeared and my mother's hair blew long behind her in the wind. Our feet were bare and our bodies pelted themselves into the sea and onto the mud flats. We revelled. We rolled and shouted and forgot that we were modern children sent from the heavens to scandalize The Aunts.

My parents stood together on the beach kissing, and my brother and I ran around them hooting. It was not a mortification here. After all, no one could see them. No one at all could see us but the gulls and the mussels.

We were complete, ecstatic, wind-wrapped, and gloriously free.

§

Later arrivals, without The Aunts, never possessed the freedom of those triumphant leapings with my windy family at Indian Point.

The Othello *Trap*

The last summer at the shore, before my brother
was born, I was reading *Othello* to impress everyone.
Actually, being nine and three quarters, I was not so
much reading it as ostentatiously leaving it lying
around. Carefully placed in front of the areas
inhabited by grownups. I left it with my turquoise
Cher bookmark displayed so anyone looking would
know the book was mine.

Mom and Dad were on the beach, just turning
back for the cottage when I found the perfect place
to put *Othello*. They couldn't miss it when they
came up to the cottage.

They were the victims of most of my
attention-getting ploys this week. They were driving
me crazy. They wandered around holding hands and
looking frantic or bedazed. The Aunts watched the

great bulk of my mother as my father helped her in and out of chairs and over door sills. They tutted and shook their heads about her pregnancy. They stopped talking as my parents came into rooms. I too hated this baby, this nebulous being that so mesmerized my parents. I competed with it, saw it as a rival, a stranger, an opponent.

I would join battle with Shakespeare on my side. "Words are power," my father said. I crept outside to set the *Othello* trap. The well box, which stood about forty feet in front of the cottage, between the lawn and the cliff, was the perfect place.

The well box was a wooden platform built up around the well to stop it from washing out in the winter storms. It had a forbidden quality. Aunt Byrd had told me about a little girl who once opened a well-box lid to look inside. She fell in and was drowned, and no one looked for her in time because they thought she had been better brought up than to go looking into well boxes.

The gist was that I was allowed to sit on the well box but never to open it. When I climbed onto it, I sat and imagined bloodied fingers scratching the boards underneath me. Today, though, I had other plans.

I climbed up and opened *Othello* to the handkerchief part. I draped the bookmark seductively between the pages, closed the book and waited. I hunkered down on top of the well box pretending to be asleep in the sun. From my perch, with my hair pulled right across my eyes, I could watch Mom and Dad walking up the shore.

They were walking slowly, my mother laughing and picking her way over the sandstones with pregnant effort. My father's face was hidden by the ball cap he wore to keep from burning. From time to time he'd stop to lift her down from a higher sandstone ridge she'd walked onto or over a piece of driftwood she could easily have stepped across herself. Then, just before the three sandstone steps that led from the beach to the grass in front of the cottage, he actually picked her up in his arms and turned with her in a long slow circle. I could hear her laughter as she began to slip down gently to the sand. She grabbed his cap on the way down and then sat in the sand, wearing the cap, giggling and holding her hand out to him to help her up. I was furious. Last summer they told me I was too heavy to toss up in the air and catch, but he had twirled her around and she was way bigger than me. All they ever did was goof around and talk about lucky accidents and hold hands, even in front of The Aunts.

I watched them from behind the well box, kicking my toes into the tall grass and sticking my tongue out in their direction, half hoping to get caught. Just as I was adding a secret and horrible face to my daring, I saw that he was ignoring the hand she held out to him and holding his arm above the elbow. I wondered if he'd been stung. Bitten by a horsefly. He pulled at his collar a bit, still rubbing his arm and took three or four fluttery steps back towards the water. He flexed his hand. Mom got all the way to her feet, still wearing the cap, not laughing now.

The screen door creaked and slammed behind me. One of the Aunts came out and called my name. I ignored her voice and watched my mother stretch out her hand for my father. He reached to take it, let it go and dropped slowly into the sand beside her. I watched him fall for a long, still time, now out of my sight in the tall grasses and wild rose bushes at the edge of the shore, while the world around me erupted into sudden sound and movement. My Aunt Maud called my father's name and ran towards the sand. My mother moved forward to him and also dropped down and out of my sight. Aunt Maud slid down the bank to them and then also dropped out of my range of vision. I stayed exactly where I was, the wind blowing my hair into my mouth while sand scattered across the cover of *Othello*. I did not move until Aunt Maud came running back towards the cottage and picked me up by the elbow, pulling me with her as she ran inside. Uncle K, sitting in isolation in the rocker beside the door, was given my arm and told to take me into the sunporch and to keep me there, no matter what.

Aunt Maud finished on the phone, shouted for The Aunts to make tea, grabbed some quilted blankets and ran back to the sand. I sat in the porch smelling the dust and musty tang of my Uncle K, his hand solid over mine.

"She'll get it all straightened around," he nodded, squeezing my hand once, warm and close.

My elbow felt heavy and a little warm where Aunt Maud had pulled it. No matter what, I thought, no matter what. Uncle K nodded gently at me several times as we listened to The Aunts' voices, indistinct from each other, worry-soft, organizing pots of tea and milk and sugar.

An easterly wind tortured the shore grasses into dance as the cars came and my mother got into the RCMP cruiser with my father's sand-covered body. I watched them from the door of the porch, through the cottage and through the blue screen door. I could see the water and the lawn and The Aunts through the windows at the end of the sunporch. I sat in a glass box on the side of the cottage watching everything, and listening to the voices above me and to the long unhinging wind.

"Ambulances take too long," my Aunt Maud said aloud. I didn't know who she was talking to, who anyone was talking to, or what they were saying. I only knew no one was saying anything to me.

The cruisers flickered their lights across the lawn and the cottage and across my Uncle K as he sat beside me. Flickers of blue on warm flannel plaid. The Aunts stood on the lawn and together, as a chorus, nodded once.

Uncle K gave me a peppermint from deep inside the dust folds of his trousers. He pushed it along his leg, near his knee, to dust it off. I took it from his hand. It was cool against the tightness of my throat. Uncle K said nothing.

He sat, as he always did, with his knees apart,

his forearms resting on his thighs, his back rounded and bent forward at the shoulders and his head cocked slightly to one side. His hands hung folded between his solid legs. He did not speak often because he stuttered — stuttered with everyone but children. He was never afraid with us; in some ways he was regarded as one of us, a larger and more awkward child. We waited in the hot silence of the porch to be called back in.

§

Aunt Maud came inside after the RCMP cruiser left for town. "Your mother will call from the hospital," she told me. "Be a big girl."

She moved back into the cottage, bustling towards the kitchen.

I did not know then about the manic activity that is a reaction to fear and grief. I hadn't heard of protecting children from information. I didn't really understand that my father was Aunt Maud's little brother, and that she was closer to him than The Aunts were.

I did not know that they had ever fought and parted over pride. I didn't have a brother then, and didn't understand that quiet bond. I didn't know that she had taught him piano scales or had let him drive her first car or that she had punched the boy who took his ball-glove in grade six. I knew only the simplest bits of their history. It never occurred to me that she might be afraid, and at that busy moment I hated her.

Uncle K nodded to me and took out cigarette bits to roll among his curling fingers; tobacco blended with peppermint. The cool of the peppermint was something I could taste, believe in as a way not to cry.

I deliberately slammed the door as I went out to the veranda to wait for the phone to ring. They would call me and then they would come and get me and we could all go home and forget this stupid place.

The last of the afternoon sun had begun curling into the sea; shards of light cut into the barn roofs on the Amherst shore. The wind had come up and the air was turning chill. I could hear my Aunt Maud's feet on the boards behind me as she came to check on me from inside the windows. I ignored her.

The tide had begun to pull its way out and my flesh was goose-skinned by the time the phone rang its triple ring. By then I had come to a place of aching quiet — maybe a "lost place" is a better description. The phone bell sounded as loud as all the world rushing in. The screen door slammed and I was holding my aunt's skirt as she spoke into the phone above me.

"Yes," she said, "yes, of course. Which one did you see?" She sniffed. "Young doctor, then? Is there anything else we can see to?"

Her voice was crisp. She stopped to listen. I could see flour on the edge of her apron, dried, wasted flour. She smelled of the rose scent that you keep in the sock drawer. I could hear my mother's voice but not her words. My aunt spoke again above me.

They discussed things, far away and above me things. Things I was not being asked about. My father needed rest and I was not restful. My mother also needed to rest, for the baby.

Aunt Maud spoke again into the phone. "Concentrate on him and leave the child to me." My mother's voice sounded briefly and then my aunt pushed it back through the phone line and hung up.

I pinched my fingers hard with my fingernails. The purple half-moon bruises helped. They turned white and ached if I held the skin around them tight.

The voices of The Aunts began again after an appropriate waiting period. Aunt Maud went out to the lawn, where they had waited silently. The smoke from Uncle K's rolled cigarette wound in through the door of the sunporch. The salt wind whispered leaves against the kitchen window.

I sat at the table, kicking my feet against the rungs of my wooden chair. My throat was tight. My parents had left me here with The Aunts. I was hot and afraid, and my peppermint was gone completely.

Dare

We met at the lighthouse, the second week of my
exile at Indian Point. Eli, Claire, Mags and me.

The lighthouse was an unmanned replacement
for the old light, which the Whittakers had burned
down one Hallowe'en. They burned down a historic
sight, or at least a cottage, every Hallowe'en.

Before I was born they had killed a summer
family. A son and two cousins had broken into a
cottage, killed the husband and done something to
the wife that The Aunts never said out loud. The
baby had never been found. Everyone knew they
did all the wrongs of the town. Even me, and I was
one of the summer people.

Nanna Whittaker was a universal threat. She
was never seen. She did not need to be. We knew
she was evil. We knew they were all evil. She lived

with an assortment of socially unrecognizable children in the narrow house on the never-taken road to the lighthouse.

The light was built on the site of an old English fort on stolen Indian land and then, later, stolen again from the French. De-evolution, my Aunt Maud called it. Completed, she said, by a Tory government breakwater which lay there crumbling and letting in more of the sea with every passing storm.

Between the breakwater and the grassy hills there was a graveyard with a single-chain fence. There were seven grey stones there, all with faded writing. The only one you could decipher was the boy grave. If you traced your fingers over the sandstone, the letters etched their way into his age and name. "Edward James," it said, and "seventeen." I stood tracing the letters of the name that day in the wind. There was more than the usual feeling of not being alone and I turned around. Two kids stood outside the fence and watched.

"There are dead men under your feet, you know," the girl on the right stated. The other giggled. "Right where you are standing now," added the first kid.

I was taken aback. What business did she have to tell me something so obvious and have it work as such a taunt? She stood with one foot swinging a loop of chain fence. Her white shorts and her sweater had tiny blue sailboats on the bottom edges. Her white hair blew behind her towards the sea. Mine blew into my mouth and over my eyes.

My reaction to her then, that day, has remained intact over the years. I felt as if my hair was messy, my clothes were unkempt and my fingernails were dirty. I didn't know her yet, so all this mattered.

The little chubby kid beside her giggled again. It seemed to be a nervous tic.

"You are standing directly on top of their heads, right now!" White Shorts taunted.

"So?"

It was all I could think of and it rang weak even in my own ears. Chubby giggled again. She wore a pink version of the same shorts set.

As long as her mother dressed her, Mags wore pink versions of Claire. Their fathers worked together but Claire's had a title in an office. Mags always looked silly in her mother's copy wardrobes but we could never figure out why. The clothes themselves were always beautiful. Mags' father always had that same sense about him; when he took his small white boat out into the sea behind Claire's father, that impression of his having copied the wrong thing was strongest.

The folds of Chubby's clothes pulled as she giggled. She looked kind. I wanted to talk to her but this other strange, beautiful girl drew my attention somehow.

A voice from behind me moved into the wind and pushed towards them.

"They been dead so long yer probly standin' on mor'n half of 'em yerself, ya little snot."

I turned, astonished. How could anyone speak

such insolence?

Long red snakes of hair covered the face and shoulders. She was around my age but she had the immediate presence I associated only with grown women. The two of them looked at one another. Chubby giggled. If it hadn't been so irritating, I'd have giggled too. This sudden group, these two power-speakers in their high-tide circle above the gravestones. Guinevere and Morgana facing each other over the graves of men a thousand years away. White Shorts took her insolent foot off the fence and Red Snakes straightened her spine and grew taller.

I had an irrational urge, as I still sometimes do with them, to duck. To roll on the ground and crawl away beneath the webbings of their power.

Chubby looked at them and then at me and giggled. She crossed her legs and whispered that she had to pee. I remembered my own bladder and thought of the stove-boiled tea The Aunts had insisted on that morning.

Biology suspended power. Chubby and I ducked into the apple bushes at the edge of the fort.

"The worst thing about being a girl is you always get the backs of your sneakers."

We were friends easily.

We walked to join the others. They had left the sandstone graves and were standing with their backs to the breakwater at the edge of the fort. As quickly as their power had come, it had relaxed, and we all moved to sit on the grasses beside the mossy well pit.

Red Snakes, we learned later, was Elizabeth-Jean, but she would only answer to derivatives of Elizabeth. After a month she allowed us "Eli", the "i" pronounced long. I as in I.

Mags gave us gum from the store and we sat in the wind and watched the boats out on the bay. Claire's father had come up on Friday with his boat trailer and Mags' family had followed Saturday. Claire's mother was away. "Doing hospital research," she said. Mags' mother was at the cottage unpacking Tupperware.

"That's what she does at home too," Mags told us. "She makes food, packs it up, unpacks it and tries to wash spaghetti stains out of green plastic dishes."

The sun warmed my hands and the thick salt air flavoured the hair that blew into my mouth. I took my sneakers off and grabbed at moss with my toes.

"And what," Claire said to Eli, "is your mother up to today?" It was happening again — that feeling between Claire and Eli. The feeling I would come to know in bank manager meetings and parties for theatre openings. The sneer, the inference, the clever unsaid word. Tension.

"I wouldn't tell ya even if I knew or cared."

Eli dropped her words to the grass in front of Claire. She would not play mothers. She didn't have one. This wasn't said the way the divorced kids I knew said it, though. It was not an admission but a declaration. If she was going to be an oddity, she was going to do it well.

I heard a voice on the wind and it was my own. "Umm, my mother is a teacher. In a school. Well, she was, and she will go back when the baby comes and..."

I felt an urge to fill the quiet between them with anything I could think of. If you have been trained to entertain, to keep the peace, silence is a nerve-shattering enemy. It must be babbled into submission. Social training can be a mixed and awkward blessing. After some twenty-seven inane facts about my mother's class size in the public school system, I shut up. Mags giggled. The breezes flapped the sleeves of our shirts against us with the sound of whipping sails.

Claire looked out to the fathers in the sea. The scarlet triple-hulled boat pulling through the waves splashed red sunlight, splashed blood — bloodlines — onto the tiny white sailboat behind it.

"Daddy says there's a crazy old man on a rusted old bike who drives around here at night. When Daddy is sailing the trimaran he sees him. Sometimes in the middle of the night."

The casualness of the word "trimaran", used as a lifestyle and an assault, was aimed at Eli. She looked bored, but Mags winced and looked at her now uncovered toes working through the moss beside my own. I cringed at the bicycle part of the story and wished she would stop. Imagine a bike wobbling over the breakwater, less than a foot wide that surrounded the fort. Imagine it with the night winds blowing and the sea in torment. I shuddered. Claire continued.

"He's an absolute raving lunatic, Daddy says. He rides along the breakwater screaming down at the water about his old dead wife. He'll probably kill someone some day and have to be locked away."

Eli yawned. "So what, there's worse than that around. He's probly jest some ghost hangin' round to scare a little blonde snot from the cottages."

She was good. The trimaran insult was cancelled out by Eli's inference that there was only one little snot at the cottages. It let Mags off the hook and nailed Claire. They were both too good at this.

"You guys want to go up to the store?" I blurted.

I could feel the tension between them again. When babble doesn't work, my mother said, try food. Mags jumped up, thrust her shoes on and pulled out three quarters in less than thirty seconds. She must feel the tension too.

Eli pulled herself lazily to her feet, pulled a pack of matches from her pocket, tossing it high in the air and catching it easily. "I'll go with ya," she said. "I've gotta get some smokes anyways."

We stared at her. She smoked? No one I knew ever smoked before junior high except for that diabetic girl in Mrs. Daily's home room, and we all figured she was about ten years ahead of the rest of us anyway. She wore a bra, had a boyfriend in grade eight and used to leave condoms on the teacher's desk at recess. And now Eli smoked. The Aunts would have a fit. It made me feel important and stupid at exactly the same instant.

She looked down at Claire. "Want to split a pack?" she whispered.

"I'll let you know," Claire said, well after we had started walking.

It wasn't a really strong response, and it had been delayed. Eli was ahead. Claire knew it too. She looked up the road.

There were two ways into town — the short dirt road past the Whittakers' house, or the normal way, the paved road. The paved road went past the light, around a couple of farms, and looped into town. It was about ten minutes longer, but we always took it so we wouldn't have to pass the evil house. We all turned towards its safety — except Claire. She looked down at the pavement and then at Eli.

"Well, you can walk all that way if you want to, but I'm walking straight."

With an insolent swing of her hair she turned from the pavement and headed down the dirt road. We stared. OK, I thought, she's won, but there was no way we could go that way. I looked at Mags. We both looked at Eli. She broke off a match, stuck the sulphur end into her mouth and followed Claire along the red dirt road.

Mags and I looked at each other.

"No way," she said.

"I know, but we can't let them get out of sight. Whittaker's is right there!" The two of them were farther away with every panicked breath we drew. The only thing worse than letting them go at all was letting them get so far ahead that we'd have to run to catch up. We might really have to run if we walked past Whittakers'. We needed to save our energy.

"Well?"

"Maybe if we just ran past the driveway?"

I nodded. We looked up the road at the two proud backs ahead, and then we stepped onto the road. We caught up to them just in sight of Whittakers'.

They stood looking at the old, narrow house. Its tall windows looked brokenly onto the road. I think now it must have originally been an old mill building. I've seen pictures of my family's woollen mill from the twenties, and the Whittaker house echoed its tall, four-storey, narrow shape. It had the same flaked grey wooden shingles, and bits of machines strewn outside. It also mirrored the worn texture of the pictures, and their stillness.

I know that the wind blew and that the colours of sky and grass must have been present, but I can't remember the house that way. It stands in my memory like the tall grey bones of a ship left to rot in harbour. It remains a kind of snapshot, without colour or movement.

Cars and fridges and rusted metal doors covered the yard. A long black car lounged in the brown grass, sifting its way into the ground with all the other metal skeletons. From the tallest window at the left of the house we saw a clothesline stretching down to attach itself to the nearest rust-wounded fender. Sepia-coloured shirts and abandoned work pants hung tattered towards the earth. They had clawed wickedly at the winds once, I thought, but now they were still.

We caught up to Claire and Eli, who were looking at the house through a clump of leaning pines on the nearer side of the driveway. We watched for a while in silence.

"OK," whispered Claire. "Walk or run?" She meant past Nanna Whittaker's driveway.

"What about after?" I asked.

"Run to town," begged Mags.

Claire looked at us. "OK," she said, "we just walk the driveway, but we do it alone."

We looked at Eli. She smiled and spat her match out on the road. "I go last."

She'd done it again. Last was most dangerous because you could be grabbed from behind as the others ran to town. The only worse place was first because of the unknown risk.

We looked at Claire. She turned towards the road and walked. She had the right to lay conditions because she was going first, but she didn't. She just went. Mags and I held hands and watched her walk.

She made it all the way to the opposite clump of pines before she ran. She had set a long walk for the rest of us. Mags and I looked to the house. Now it was time for one of us to go.

"Sarah and I could walk at the same time but a few feet apart," said Mags. We looked at Eli.

"Sure," she said. Her contest was not with us. Mags started out about twenty steps ahead of me. When she was half-way across the driveway, I started, clutching a pine needle with me from the trees we had hidden in.

I don't remember looking at the house, but I must have. I have enough of an impression of the place that I must have been staring. I imagined faces looking out of the broken windows, and I saw bodies hanging from cords in doorways. The voices of The Aunts began to sound their stories in my head.

One of the girls had hanged herself over a baby, I knew that. There was a retarded son who ate from cans, I knew. There was a cousin who'd escaped from jail, and everyone knew he was living on the welfare with his old, fat mother. Nanna had a still and made screech during Prohibition. She fermented blood in her still along with the liquor, they said, and that was why it sold so well to the kind of evil devils who drank away the Christian goal of temperance. The kids ran naked in the house and never ate solid food. Nanna spent all her baby bonus money on a satellite dish for the TV and hid the dish behind the house where she buried her dead children. I knew all of this from The Aunts and their friends who came together to play bridge and speak the village truths.

I heard every accusation of violence against them as I walked the dirt road beside their house. I must have been staring, because when I got to the trees where we were free to run to town I realized that I could clearly see my Uncle K's bicycle.

It was naked in the sun, leaning against the sodden pile of wood that formed makeshift steps to the Whittaker veranda and front door. Above the bicycle, in the frame of a crooked window, I could see his arm and the outline of his jaw as he brought a dark brown bottle to his lips. I registered the bike, I saw him lean forward to speak to someone in the room and I turned around to look at Eli. She smiled and gave me a lazy thumbs-up as I approached the free mark where I could run. When she got here she would know. She would see the bike. She would walk past as I did, and see the bike and the arm of my Uncle K drinking blood with Nanna Whittaker. She would see, she would know, and she would tell the others.

Claire and Mags had both looked straight ahead as they walked by. They wouldn't have seen anything, and they wouldn't recognize my Uncle K's bike anyway. But Eli was from here and she would know, and she would tell and then all three of them would understand that the crazy old man at the lighthouse screaming on his bicycle was Uncle K. I felt the pressure of the trees leaning with me into the wind, pushing me to run. I felt the dust from the road catch in my throat as I kicked it up and ran.

§

By the time I got to the store, Claire and Mags had Popsicles melting in their hands. I waited on the steps for Eli and my fate. I looked at her as she walked up the steps and she smiled directly into my eyes. My desperate dreams of her not seeing the bike leaning in the sunlight were shattered. She knew and now, before going into the store, she turned to face the others. She looked at Claire. This was it. I waited.

Eli pointed at me on the steps where I was catching my breath from the run to town.

"She walked slower than you did, even if ya did go first and get farther, snotface."

She smiled sweetly at Claire and walked into the store. Mags giggled and Claire grinned.

"Some people can't take defeat." She smiled knowingly at both of us and nibbled her purple flavour.

I was dizzy with relief as I went inside. I reached into the cooler beside Eli, wondering if I should thank her. She solved the problem for me.

"Forget it," she said into the ice-cream section of the freezer. "That little snottola don't need to know a thing. She don't know nothing now. Why change it?"

I was crawling out of the orange Popsicle box when Mrs. Wilson's voice sounded through the store to her sales clerk at the cosmetics. "Nancy," it said, "Nancy-Lynn, you mind now. I saw that Lizabeth-Jean Whittaker come in here just a minute ago, and I don't see her now. Don't you sell her cigarettes if you do see her. If you don't see her, keep looking until you do, and then don't you take your eyes off her. A Whittaker is a Whittaker right down to the bone."

Eli froze. I got up as quickly as I could, making all the noise I could, to pretend I hadn't heard.

Eli was a Whittaker.

No wonder she had walked so slowly past the house. She had cheated. I thought of her gift of the bike to me. Well, she hadn't come up with the dare. Claire had, and she hadn't said you couldn't be a Whittaker and take the challenge. What did Eli feel like as we all walked past her house in fear? Had anyone watched from inside as she walked past? How would it feel to have your children so ashamed of who you are? I thought about the bent arm in the window. Had my Uncle K been watching as I walked past him with the summer people's children?

Mrs. Wilson smiled at me, but I ignored her as she took my money. Eli crouched in the cooler until I left the store. I got outside finally, with my Popsicle dripping orange into its paper bag.

"Where are your smokes?" Claire asked Eli when she came out.

"Where's your money for half the pack?" she answered.

It lacked the zing of before. She looked at me, waiting.

I glanced back over my shoulder into the store. Mrs. Wilson was looking out; The Aunts would certainly hear that I had been there. She looked away distastefully, noting Eli there beside me.

"She don't know nothing now. Why change it?" I said, returning the gift of anonymity, as much as we could exchange in front of windows.

Claire and Mags looked at us both.

"Don't know what?" Mags asked, because

Claire had refused to acknowledge her curiosity.

Eli grinned and reached into her pocket. "She don't know that I stole a pack of Bazooka Joe for all of us 'stead of just myself this time. Since you walked the farthest, snot, you get first choice."

Eli handed the gum to Claire and then to us and we walked back towards the lighthouse, to watch the sea till the suppertimes of our differing worlds were called.

Kiss

I was in trouble with the family.

Again.

I'd been out wandering the beach and had arrived just as The Aunts were on their way up the shore road, over the rocks and home. Even the bridge ladies had gone home. It was late afternoon, and I'd missed the luncheon.

The Aunts nodded to me as if I were a stranger to whom they nodded on the way to church. Little recognition was accorded to people on Sundays; it was the day of greater thoughts. Missing the luncheon, where I was supposed to pour the tea, was not as bad as most of the things my Uncle K had done, but it was still not good. I was finally in disgrace for real — but this time it was worth it.

I heard the floor creak under my feet as I walked over the veranda boards towards the blue screen door. I could see Aunt Maud clearing up the last of the paper napkins and the scorecards from the bridge hands. It took me a thousand years to go inside the cottage.

My mouth was burning from illicit kisses under the lighthouse steps. I was late without a good excuse. I did not think the event of my first kiss, and my first grope, would get much celebration or understanding. It definitely would not be a good excuse. I was sure that I was in a whole lot of trouble for being late, and I was elated.

I would tell them nothing. Whatever they did to me, I'd keep my secret. I would take my scandalous, delicious secret to the grave. It would be that: the active and deliberate clasping of a secret against my heart into death and beyond! It was not a passive act, I decided, but a triumphant one.

I was late, I'd been caught in the act by my Uncle K, and I'd been caught at being my Uncle K's grand-niece by the summer boy from Lake Muskoka.

That was the real summer place, Claire said, even more than her father could afford. If you summered in Ontario at Lake Muskoka you had it made, Mags' father said. Made in the shade. Lake water was richer than ocean water. Bloodsuckers were better than jellyfish. Lake people had it made.

And I'd been caught by him and with him. Caught with Chester Oliver of Lake Muskoka. And made late too, so that I missed pouring the stove-boiled tea for The Aunts at bridge. I shivered, I sniffled, I savoured every step as I ran home in my first hormonal disgrace.

Chester Oliver could belch louder than any boy at the point that summer.

Claire watched him from under her hair, pretending not to. It has always been her elegant way of hunting.

Eli spat scornfully when he sauntered by. Normally she treated any boy she hadn't beaten up with cruel, indifferent sniffs. Those she bested in fights she treated as weaker but respected friends. I'd never before seen her notice anyone enough to spit.

Mags giggled nervously, pretending not to understand him, when he stopped to talk to us.

I pretended nothing. I was in love. I had never met anyone so arrogant and so wonderful in my life. Well, not anyone taller than me.

Chester was called Chet. I don't think I could love a man with such a name today. My friends at school would later prance around and call each other Chet, Chas, Tad and Biff in order to belittle the kids they met at college — kids with boats and portfolios and monosyllabic, preppy names. All the blond and golden kids who brought sweaters and bobbed haircuts to the Maritimes.

Once I admitted that I had loved a man named Chet, and they called me Buffy for a month. Never mind. Chester Oliver was my first love, and he taught me how to spit even farther than Eli and my Uncle K together.

He was all of a long, low whistle and a smooth

walk by.

He spat and hit the lighthouse.

Claire looked obviously away, Mags said, "Gross," and Eli lit a smoke. I never heard her call them cigarettes. The smooth walk stopped.

Long look.

"Why don't you ladies take a picture? It lasts longer."

"How do you spit so far?" I asked him.

"Come here, little girl, and I'll show you how it's done."

I got up immediately, surprising us all. We climbed the lighthouse steps; he explained that this would help prevent backwash. Backwash, he said, was when you spat into the wind and it hit your face. This was the absolute worst that could happen in spitting, he said. You wasted your gob that way.

Once he started to teach me, he became a person. He was still lovely, still elegant and still possessed of the most startling movement I had ever been drawn to, but he was human.

Whenever men are teaching, they relax. For a long time I'd let them teach me my own name if I thought it would relax them. It's not till later that you learn to teach each other.

He taught me how to hang my head and collect the drool. He taught me how to bunch my spit between my teeth. He taught me how to wedge my tongue behind my teeth and push. He was patient with the long, wet, silver line that connected my mouth to the ground the first few times. He was patient with the nondirectional lobbies, patient even when he stood downwind of me and collected my undisciplined effort on his narrow face.

He was patient until the late afternoon, until my friends had left for supper. I remember being a little afraid, not of him but of how beautiful he was. I don't remember climbing down the lighthouse steps and under the platform with him, but I must have. That is where my first kiss happened.

That is where we lay shivering from being suddenly in shadow on the cold earth, where the shade stopped the grass from growing. That is where, suddenly shy and stupid, he acted as if we were down there only for the sights underneath the lighthouse steps. Peeling grey paint, traveller's moss and bare red earth.

He belched loud, long belches. "Smell burps and yell burps," he called them. "Come in all shapes and sizes."

We pretended to tickle each other for a while. He seemed to need to pretend that this was something else. I was curious and a little impatient. Finally I kissed him, because it seemed silly not to. That was why I had come down here in the first place. It seemed practical to me. He seemed embarrassed. Surprised. I could feel all this in his shoulders and in the pull against his jeans.

It must be so embarrassing to boys, I thought, to have everything going on in their minds and bodies be so obvious. They didn't get to keep much private. I would hate to have everything that clear to anyone who looked. I could understand his embarrassment, with his body giving him away like that, but not his surprise. I didn't realize that in his understanding I was supposed to be reluctant and shy.

We rolled on the ground, and for a while my foot stuck out from underneath the steps. I felt the sun on my black sneaker. Absorbing light, I remembered from science class, and then that fragment of the concrete world, outside sensation was lost.

When he pulled me on top of his long thin body, other fragments whispered and were buried and replaced.

Heightened whispers.

Sun, shadow, twig under the elbow, sea in my ears, sandstone graves at eye level just across the grass. Never seen them this way....

I turned beneath him and the fragments changed. I remembered some of the things I had heard from Claire, seen on TV, read in magazines. It was difficult to sort out the things I'd been taught from the things I was feeling. For instance, I knew I was supposed to feel overpowered, vulnerable, pressured, bashful. I didn't think I was supposed to feel intrigued, powerful, or compassionate towards this shaking boy. I was supposed to close my eyes, I remembered. Why? What wasn't I supposed to see? I felt rock under my left shoulder, Chet's hands moved, should I stop them? I was supposed to want to stop them, I recalled. What weren't they supposed to do? Would I decide to find out? His breath was ragged and his mouth was soft and hard, both at the same time. Same mouth as spit, I thought, same mouth as belches. Loudest anywhere. I kissed back closer and further away and closer again. It was all kind of mesmerizing and foggy and curious. I thought we were supposed to be adversaries, not like this. This was all sort of reaching and pulling and ... *observed.*

Uncle K.

Uncle K looking under the steps, looking in and seeing me. He leaned down from his bicycle, peering through the spokes, and we looked up at his hat; it blocked the sun out with a shapeless grey-fedora cloud.

He opened his long narrow throat and hollered.

He did not stutter.

The holler continued until we were away, out of his sight, running fast in decently opposite directions.

§

Chester ran well. He got away and left for Ontario with his parents the next week. This was not related to lighthouse indiscretions; his family visit was simply at its end. I was not free to see him go. I was grounded for a week for missing the pouring of the tea. I even had to miss my Monday walk with Uncle K, who was made to come in and tell me so himself. He stood in the sunporch door, where The Aunts could hear him and see me, and passed me a linty peppermint telling me it was not for "f-freshening my b-breath" and laughing so uproariously at his own joke that The Aunts shooed him out of the cottage. They tutted to one another about candy and spoiled constitutions as we watched him pedal out of the dooryard, down the lane way and back towards the town.

II Guardians

Before the First Cup

I explain to James, while he is sleeping in the
sunporch and cannot think me odd, that I have
always hated Sundays, and not because of Church.
Aunt Maud said she was a hopeful agnostic, more
for my sake than her own, so she never made me
walk through the blueberry bluff at the end of the
path to the little square Presbyterian church where
Aunt Byrd played the organ and Aunt Wynd ran the
Sunday-school and Uncle K was whispered about at
the tea after the service while he bicycled the town
chuckling with the barn swallows in the sun.
Sundays for Mags and Claire meant good shoes and
drives to church in Claire's father's Oldsmobile.
They were Anglican. For Eli, whose God was one of
splendid isolation, Sunday was a day to sit on the
dock and watch the lobster boats bob against the

creosote-covered beams below her, while the fishermen spent the day either in church or eating turkey suppers with their families.

I began hating Sundays at the cottage because of all the phone calls from home. Each phone call was the same. The phone would ring our ring on the party line, two shorts and a long, and Aunt Maud would speak softly with my mother and then hold the phone against her chest before I had the chance to talk. She'd look at me and whisper, "Don't upset your mother. Your dad's better, but still in ICU", or "your dad's better, but they're keeping him for observation", and later, "your dad's at home. The nurse is very nice." Aunt Maud's quiet warning "don't upset your mother" was always prefaced in conversation with my mother by frightening medical words I couldn't understand and couldn't ask about. My family was raised, generations of it, to not upset our mothers.

Something about the cottage world kept me wrapped in its rules, so I never asked questions of my mother and never provided anything but cheerful stories about spruce gum or cookies from the store. When I talked to her I could hear caution in her voice, telling me my dad was better, the nurse was nice, and, later, that there was a baby now, two weeks late and bigger than I had been at birth, born the day my father left the ICU. Her voice was tired and quiet, holding back. I heard it every Sunday evening on the phone and remembered it at night, lying awake and listening to the walls creak and the ocean slither on the night-black beach. I still hate the hours of isolation from the rest of the world when it's time to sleep on Sunday nights, waiting for it to be Monday.

On Mondays Uncle K came by with strawberries, or maple-walnut ice-cream or a stick of driftwood for the Franklin stove, and we'd walk up to the fort or to the point. He'd tell me what the other men were up to or how there needed to be rain for the blueberries soon or how the lobster season looked like it was shaping up. We watched sandpipers and looked at the highwater mark, imagining winter storms or skipped flat stones out into the bay. Mondays were good days at the shore, with all the quiet of Sundays, but none of the ache of waiting for the phone.

When I started apprenticing as a stage manager, I felt blessed by Sundays for the first time because they were days for matinées and evening shows, hard-working days with paper work and sweeping floors and keeping homesick actors happy. Mondays are the day off in my current world, which is one of the reasons I continue here, making coffee, ordering pizza and watching the pretend worlds unfold in the rectangle of light at the centre of the theatre.

This Monday, here again, I am content. James has emerged from under the orange wool blanket and the apple-leaf spread. He is in the kitchen making coffee. I can smell it blending with the autumn scent of mud coming up through the earth. Mud winds, we called it, the underneath reek of rotting weed and salt.

The cranes are out on the flats today. Summer is ending, autumn beginning. At Indian Point these seasons join for a week. The cranes have always stopped for this one week to feed in the shelter of our bay. Today, as the wind bites through my sweater, I am remembering the tall blue cranes and these strange and blended weeks.

Cranes, mud winds, coffee and the smell of Absorbine liniment.

Liniments

Eli and I were going out to break into cottages. We had a screwdriver and a flat piece of plastic that we had found in the dirt of the main road. We had a hammer wrapped in a towel that was held in place by elastic bands; this would muffle any sounds of breaking glass. I had three peanut-butter sandwiches from The Aunts in my pocket, and Eli had a bottle of Alpine beer from her cousin. Mags and Claire had gone back to their cities.

Eli said it didn't surprise her that they had hightailed it out of here at the first sign of a cold wind. Summer people started getting cold in August and none of them ever lasted past September 5. She made me feel thick-blooded and real, better than the summer people because I had relatives in town. She gave me one of her cigarettes. I used up a book of matches lighting it in the wind, but she didn't offer to light it for me. She pretended that I was doing it easily. It was a quiet day of friendship and accepting lies.

I didn't tell her that my parents were coming in a week and that my father was fine; I felt she liked me better when he lay in the hospital, so in our conversations that was where he stayed. I didn't tell her that I now had a brother, that my family was now more perfect. I kept my mother pregnant.

It was undignified to be pregnant. "Knocked up", we called it, "a bun in the oven", "up the stump". It was passive and weak and it was done to you because you were a woman. We were unaware of power. We were unaware, or maybe afraid, of our ability to choose such a deep connection to the earth and to each other. Women who were pregnant were ridiculous, and women who did not have children were dangerous. We were taught by GI Joe and Barbie. GI Joe had boots and could sit on a plastic Johnny West horse or in a rugged jeep. Barbie had pumps and her legs wouldn't open far enough for her to sit astride a plastic Ken doll, let alone a horse.

We were taught that pregnancy was, at the very least, a shameful and awkward ordeal. The only thing worse than being pregnant yourself was having a pregnant mother; mothers were supposed to be beyond these things. My mother's pregnancy lowered me in Eli's eyes. I was to be pitied, and this was important. I was lucky and privileged, and I was sure that Eli would hate me if she knew that my mother had passed through her disgrace and into renewed motherhood. On this day of break-ins I wanted to be liked and respected by Eli more than ever. Soon it would be over, and I wanted to be real friends today.

We got into the first cottage by taking off the padlock hasp on the front door. Eli said they had left us an invitation by screwing a hasp to a door like that. I watched her freckled wrist turning as she pulled the metal piece away from the door. We looked at the still-locked padlock on the useless metal arm and giggled. Then Eli pushed the door open and we went inside.

We looked inside the kitchen and then went back to the door. Eli walked around in the dark and called things out to me.

"My brothers always lighted fires when they did this. They got caught once. Someone saw the smoke coming out the window."

We split the beer she had brought, and we sat on the cold floor in the dark and ate my sandwiches. Eli told me how her cousins would party all winter in one cottage and leave the mess for the rich people to find in the spring. She said you could break whatever you wanted, and they'd just buy new things the next summer.

There was a photograph on the top bookshelf opposite the door. It was a foggy picture of an old man with a dog sitting on a chair in front of the cottage we were in. The grandfather, I thought. I tried not to look at it as Eli told me what her brothers and cousins had done to cottages along the shore.

She went back to the kitchen and came out with a small blue coffee mug. "You have to take something too," she said. I didn't want to move. She said it again, as if I hadn't understood her: "You have to take something from the cottage too." The coffee mug had a name on it, and chips under the handle. "Bob's," it said. It belonged to Bob. Maybe he was the grandfather in the picture. Eli was waiting.

"Couldn't we just leave the beer bottle here in the middle of the floor?" I asked. "That would be a mess." She looked at me. I'd missed the point, I could see that in her expression.

"Do what you want," she said, bored and scornful. She walked outside without shutting the door. Such stupidity didn't merit a slam.

When I came out, she asked me what I had taken, and I held out the picture. "Great," she said. "Stuff like that means a lot to those people, so they notice it right away."

That was the point, then — to hurt the people who could afford to spend their summers at the sea.

At the next place I didn't go inside. Eli pried a shutter away and came out with a piece of driftwood with painted shells glued all over it. I had made something like that for my Aunt Maud once. The picture in its frame bumped against my leg and weighed down my pocket as I walked behind her.

§

The next cottage had a garden shed beside it. The shed was painted red and had glass windows without shutters. The cottage matched the shed and also had glass windows. Eli began to circle the cottage, and I saw her reaching for her hammer.

I could not do this again.

I called to her and told her that it would be better to go inside the shed. She ignored me so I began to take the lock off the door. If I got in first and called her, I knew she would follow me and not go inside the cottage right away. Maybe after that I would think of some way to make her stop without her hating me.

She paused to watch. She was standing close behind me as I opened the shed door. She was far enough away, though, to run when the wasps began to swarm around my face and hair. She screamed and ran towards home along the old fort road.

I have never since been able to hear the sound of stinging insects without jumping up, without nausea. By the time I got to the cottage my eyes had swollen shut. My lips were thick and my hair was filled with screaming pain. Aunt Maud and Uncle K were sitting on the veranda watching the cranes out on the mud flats; he always came to the shore to watch the birds feed in the last of summer.

When they saw me, I was dragged into the water and submerged in the closest tidal pool by Maud's strong hands. When she went in to get blankets for the drive to the doctor, my Uncle K took over. He rolled me through wet beach sand, rinsed it away again, and pulled a bottle out of his coat pocket. The cool of the Absorbine liniment for horses covered my body. The stench and the relief were both overpowering and instant.

I was wrapped in blankets and taken to the doctor, with the comforting reek of horse-strength liniment surrounding my body. The doctor gave me a shot and much later I woke up, in Aunt Maud's flannel nightgown, on the couch by the window of our cottage. The autumn night winds had come up. The windows beside me rattled slightly. A birch fire was crackling in the Franklin stove. This room was the warmest and most secure place in all the world. It was home. Uncle K was sipping tea, I could hear his mouth sounds on the tea mug. Aunt Maud was reading.

On the table beside me they had placed two things. One was a bottle of Absorbine liniment. The other was a small framed picture of an old man and his dog sitting in front of a family cottage that now stood open not far down the shore.

When Uncle K and I took our Monday walk that week it was a quiet one. He carried a hammer and nails and two squares of scrap wood and I carried a screwdriver and the photograph. My throat ached and my chest was tight from the silence with him. Twice, when I tried to explain how hard it was to stand up to Eli, he shook his head. When we stopped at the O'Brian cottage, identified for me quietly by Aunt Maud, Uncle K stood with his back to me as I crept in, placed the picture back on its shelf in the chilly darkened room and came outside again.

I stood, also quiet and facing away, as I heard the blows of the hammer attach the wooden square to the outside wall and the creak as the screwdriver turned the new screws and the restored padlock hasp went home. "Safe as any place can be," he stuttered, "from the kind of kids we got around here," and, still not looking at me, he picked up his tools and started down the lane towards the McKenzie's shed.

Breakwater

The evening Eli broke her ankle jumping off the breakwater was the evening I met Nanna Whittaker.

§

I was setting red clay cranes to dry on the veranda boards in the late afternoon when Uncle K whistled to me from the beach. He shook his head when I answered him with my usual hello yell and motioned to me urgently from the sand. Aunt Maud was inside reading. I could see her pool of light, yellow and warm, around the wooden rocker by the fire.

The Aunts were rattling plates at each other in the kitchen. Rattling plates also at the messy condition of Aunt Maud's kitchen. "Now if your mother, our sister, were here, you would never catch the place in such a state. No, bless her heart, she would have kept it up much better," the rattles implied.

Aunt Maud and I had spent the day reading. We had made Rice Krispies squares for lunch at around two and had existed in peace until The Aunts came by to visit. The kitchen was littered with marshmallow and buttered bits of wax paper.

The Aunts were scandalized by disorder. In their day mess had been the first sign of a mind growing idle. Women whose kitchens went to the devil were soon to follow. Sloppiness was not only ungodly, it was madness. They scooped up evidence of human failing wherever they saw it thickening. They picked up cups before you had finished the tea or coffee in them.

They ironed sheets.

They cleared off tables under your resting arms.

They starched doilies.

My Aunt Maud generally left them to clean her littered kitchen and went to read. She did not see any particular point in being viewed as a competent adult, so she smiled and went away. She was tolerant and put up with my thirteenness as well as she handled The Aunts. She climbed into her books and refused to take offence at a foolish world.

Not having learned her tolerance, I sat outside. That was why I heard my uncle's whistle just above the kitchen chatter. He whistled and leaned, hiding, out from behind the well box on the shore. "Eli has fallen. She wants your helping," he whispered.

He disentangled himself from the metal wheels and we walked up the beach towards the breakwater. "W-wounded robins want helping," he said once, softly. He smiled and looked out into the rising tide.

§

Eli was curled in a pool of salt water behind the sandstone rocks at the bottom of the breakwater. Her body was tiny, reduced. Her arrogance was in suspension, and her lips in the cold of the evening were purple around her cigarette. I looked up at the grey cement wall above us. The ragged, stony path of the breakwater hung over our heads. Eli had walked that broken way all her life and had never fallen before.

Her ankle was blue; blue and bruised on her skinny leg. At thirteen Eli looked as skinny as she had at nine. I had envied her that, but I did not tonight. Uncle K's scarf and one suspender were wrapped around the tiny leg. Two bits of driftwood stick splinted the bones together.

She did not look up.

I put my sweater around her and began to shiver in the dusk. Uncle K lifted her bones into his arms and nodded at his bicycle. I picked it up from the rocks and followed them along the beach until we came to a tear in the breakwater and climbed through to the fort and up over the grass. We walked down the road to Whittakers' with the crickets and the shore-birds sounding all around us.

The Whittakers' grey house was dark against the closing sky. Eli still said nothing. She hung limp, but from time to time the fist that hung down my uncle's back stretched its fingers out and then reshaped itself. Clenched, then tautly extended, then clenched again as we stepped into the Whittaker yard.

Nanna opened the door. She looked at Eli's ankle and at the purple of her lips and began to talk above me, to Uncle K. She looked only at him, talked only to him. She ignored Eli and seemed not to see me at all. She asked Uncle K what Eli had said about something that had happened yesterday. She pinched out a smile and told him Eli tended to exaggerate. Then she asked what Eli might have said about her cousin. Eli knew what was happening, I could see that. But she drifted.

That's what I called it. Whenever something was happening above her, Eli drifted. Sometimes she even hummed. It happened when she couldn't win. She was drifting now, not looking at any of us. I stood there on the steps behind Uncle K, wondering why all this strangeness surrounded Eli's fall.

The Aunts would have had me inside taking Aspirin, enveloping me in fuss, if this had been me. I hid my scraped knees because I couldn't stand all the flapping that was part of injury in my family. Even tiny bruises were examined and worried over. I couldn't find a way to understand this Whittaker reaction.

Eli looked around once, when Nanna mentioned one of the boys, Eli's oldest cousin. Then she drifted again and curled back into my Uncle K. I put the bicycle against the steps, where I'd seen it once before, and followed them inside.

We went into the darkened summer kitchen and then passed farther in. Uncle K put Eli down on a tufted brown couch and pulled it closer to the stove. He pulled a blanket off the kitchen door and tucked it gently around Eli. He picked some papers off the floor and began to build a fire. I stood in the corner that the door made with the wall and hoped that I would not have to understand any of this: this cold, grey place, the injuries here, this huge woman's pleading.

Nanna stood beside a cradle by the window and looked at my Uncle K. Her dress hung loose at the bottom, but fit the bulk of her body tightly across her belly and thighs. Its pattern of vines and dirty leaves rustled in the whining draft of the place. She had a shawl wrapped around her and she wore men's slippers on her feet.

The cradle held a thousand dolls, all of them leaning just far enough back that their movable eyes were slitted open and suspended; wounded children in a cradle, with clinging eyes and twisted plastic lips. They were sinister in the shadows behind her green print dress.

Nanna looked at Eli and at my uncle's working back, and crossed to a table to pour something out of a vinegar bottle into a glass. Uncle K stopped to take the glass and crossed the floor to

Eli. He touched her lip to the glass and nodded at her to drink.

Nanna moved her great print dress around the room. She stooped to pick up a child's crayon drawings from the floor and looked at Eli. She stood under the lightbulb of that room and held out the paper for a while, offering it somehow. Eli closed her eyes and shut us out. Nanna dropped her shoulders.

She saw me in the doorway. "What in hell are you lookin' at? Get your arse over to the road and get the nurse to come."

"D-doctor," whispered Uncle K, and smiled at me. I bolted to begin the run to town.

§

Eli and I never spoke of that night. Not everyone is taught to share. Not everyone who lives through events wants to make their healing public. Survival can need its privacy for years. I think my uncle wanted me to see that as we walked home beside the bay.

He soft-pedalled his bicycle all the way down the road to the cottage, and I walked beside him. The moon came up over the water and the whitecaps smoothed their way into the sea. It was a lovely softened night. When we could see the lights at Indian Point, we stopped. "I don't understand," I told him.

"No," he said, "we don't all get to. We get to look, but not see too much. You leave her alone and you'll be friends; you make her tell too soon and she'll hate you." He ruffled my hair and turned away. He twisted the odd, gaunt bicycle and pedalled down the road and out of sight.

It was a long time before I understood what he had told me, but I took his advice and never spoke to Eli about the night she broke her ankle. Later on, we were friends enough to speak about survival. My Uncle K, as usual, was right.

§

Later that night, Aunt Maud had to promise the RCMP that Uncle K would never pick a fight at the Mayfair tavern again. He'd gone straight there on his bicycle, crashed open the door and heaved a chair at three of the Whittaker boys who were sitting at the bar drinking draft and playing quarters. He'd been picking up a bottle to break when Johnny jumped up from his table and dragged him out to the cruiser. Johnny said, seeing as it was Uncle K, he could go to Maud's for the night instead of the station, but he had to promise to pay for the shattered mirror above the bar.

I kept asking him why, exactly, he went after Eli's cousins and what they had done, but all he'd say on our Monday walk to the point was old and foolish as he was, Johnny should have let him be.

Nanna Talk

Nanna Whittaker told me that The Aunts had bootlegged during Prohibition. When they ran the old hotel, now the poolhall, they made special little paper bags for all the businessmen who stayed there on their way to P.E.I. The businessmen always left with a bag and a smile. This must be where the expression "in the bag" came from. "Half in the bag" must mean you were too drunk to keep your liquor hidden. The men at the tavern used these expressions, and now I knew that The Aunts were connected to them.

Nanna said The Aunts had gone out to the Thursday temperance meetings and then made their money at the Saturday dances. She said everyone knew they had to run the business themselves because the men in my family were all old drunks. Uncle K denied that his sisters had ever been near a dance, and claimed that Nanna Whittaker said these things to offend me, but they had the opposite effect. The Aunts began to be intriguing. I watched them constantly for signs of their past vices. I watched for knowing winks and significant glances on the sunporch, for visits from strange men late at night. For feather boas. I was fascinated by this wonderful gossip about them. I wanted more. They had been bad, and I liked them better.

Nanna Whittaker also told me that my Uncle K had had affairs with the woman at the bank. The woman at the bank was now the woman at the library of the seniors' home, and she had no hair. Uncle K always smiled at her as he bicycled by the huge bay windows of the home with their bright yellow trim. I didn't notice this until Nanna Whittaker began to tell me the hidden stories of my family.

After Aunt Wynd had been jilted, she'd gone away from town for almost a month. She'd come back skinnier than when she left, and she'd gone to the States. No one from this town would marry her after that. Everyone knew what that trip meant. I didn't.

Aunt Maud said that it was silly and unimaginative to gossip and that I should know better. She said people were cruel and it was always the truth they never bothered to find out about, and it was a damn shame what a small town could do to hurt a woman. All I got from this was that Aunt

Maud was angry. I still couldn't figure out what the trip was all about. I knew better than to ask again.

I told Nanna Whittaker that Aunt Maud said gossiping was cruel. Nanna Whittaker said Aunt Maud had escaped from an asylum.

Nanna said that Aunt Byrd had lorded it over everyone that she was a politician's wife but that she hadn't been so proud when her father drove them to the wedding with a shotgun.

"What did your Aunt Byrd's precious senator say to her father at his own wedding?" she asked me. This was more like a riddle than a question, because right after asking it she answered herself: "Don't shoot, sir. Please don't shoot."

The worst thing about these little conversations with Nanna Whittaker was that she'd never explain anything. When I repeated any of the things she told me, I got into trouble or, worse, I disappointed someone.

Children in my family were never beaten. Instead they were given the "disappointment treatment". It was a time-honoured tradition. My father and my Aunt Maud had themselves been disappointments, and then the family took me in hand. I was a disappointment when I was bad. I hadn't lived up to my intelligence or to my position in the community. The position in the community part was The Aunts', but even Uncle K used the disappointment technique. His variation was that I was acting foolish. If I wanted to get as mean-hearted as everyone else in this town, then he guessed it was my business, but he didn't want to stick around and listen.

I told Claire and Mags that I wished The Aunts would beat me up instead. Being locked in a closet would be easier. I would rather they knocked me across the room. Claire and Mags said it sounded better than getting spanked by the housekeeper, but at least they could get their housekeepers fired. Claire and Mags could be counted on for support.

Eli told me to shut up. I didn't know how good I had it, she said.

We didn't talk for days. I was furious that she would use her life against mine when all I was looking for was sympathy.

I had to sit on the wind-bleached steps of the Whittaker house three days in a row before Eli would forgive me for getting mad at her. I would call on her, there would be a brief wait, and then Nanna would come out instead. "I don't think she wants to see you, missie, but you can wait if you want." I usually waited about an hour and then went home. I knew she was trying to decide if I'd suffered enough shame for me to earn her friendship. Relationships with Eli have always been about things owing, about things counted up and kept track of and about exchanges.

It was during the days I spent on Eli's rickety steps, petitioning for Eli's friendship, that Nanna Whittaker began to tell me stories I didn't want to hear.

§

Claire's mother was not at a resort for the summer. She was in an alcohol clinic in Toronto. Mags' mother was spending her nights with Claire's father and, worse yet, Mags' father didn't mind. Mags' father wanted a promotion, and that was why he didn't mind. Mags' mother didn't mind spending her night-times with Claire's father because it was more interesting than sorting Tupperware.

§

Uncle K had been hunting once, so drunk he shot a rabbit with a twelve-gauge. There was rabbit fur all over him when they took him to the RCMP station to sober him up and call his sisters to come and get him. Dead rabbit everywhere.

§

Aunt Maud had been captured by the Whittaker boys, the oldest three, one Saturday in June when she was around fourteen. Everyone knew that she'd never married because no one man could ever top that afternoon for her.

Nanna Whittaker went on. She had a low, smoking voice and a scratchy wheeze when she spoke. As she hurt me on those steps in the wind, she smiled. She was telling me things because of who I was. I was a summer kid, and my family had once employed the town. She hated me for my last name as much as everyone in town hated her for hers. She was trying to hurt me, and Eli was inside waiting to see how much I'd listen to, for her.

When Nanna said the things about Aunt Maud, Eli came out and we walked to the fort. We left the steps and Nanna shouted empty gossip down the road after us as we walked away.

We didn't say much. We didn't have to. Eli had felt the gossip change to hate and she'd come outside. She understood more about hate than I did. We went to sit under the rotten apple tree at the fort, and we forgave each other.

Eli and I have hated each other at times since then but we have always, eventually, come back. We sit under that tree again, wherever we are, tasting that first forgiveness. Before we'd met I'd never been wronged, and Eli had never been treated well. We had no reason to end up being friends. We do not have any more reason now. I'm not sure how we keep finding our way back there, but we do.

Presents

Aunt Maud liked to play a game of finding presents with me. She'd tell me that there was something for me to find in the closet of her room. I'd have to go and look at one thing and then come back and describe it to her. "Brown purse on the back of the door," I'd say. "Warm," she'd say, or "Cold." Then I'd climb the wooden stairs again and find another thing to tell her about. I told her about things that I guessed might be beside the present. We mapped the contents of her closet all through the afternoons.

I never looked inside any of the boxes or pockets or packages that were stacked inside her closet. I wanted to but that was not part of the game.

The closet smelled of clothes worn at the ocean. Slightly damp; salty. All the clothes in the closet were blue. Permanent press, she called them. "Too much to do in life to spend time ironing," she said. Too many books to look at, too many unread *New Yorkers* in the basket by her chair. Too much more upstairs in the closet, waiting.

The shoes were leather or brown suede. Low, thick-heeled, flat, wide-toed. One pair of knitted slippers that she wore once the sun went down, hot or cool. They were the kind of slippers that feel as if they were knit with plastic wool. They were orange and brown and had a seam down the middle of the sole. I thought of the story of the mermaid who was cursed to walk on knives inside her shoes in exchange for legs and life on land, because she loved a mortal prince and had to pay something for her happiness. I don't know what happiness my Aunt Maud had made her sacrifices for. There were no outward signs of princes in her daily life, and there were no other rewards I could see the point of at the time.

The warm, warmer, warmest game would continue through the straw hats, around the shades of blue polyester pantsuits and under the brown, still shoes. Finally, after a hundred trips up and down the stairs and after her comment "That is the warmest you can get without combusting", I'd find it.

"It" was a book from the library wrapped in special blue tissue paper — wrapped and sealed from the air in a thick blue skin. I couldn't tell what the book was through the paper and the masking tape. She wrapped the books while walking between the library and the cottage. She took the tape and the paper with her into town and encased the package on the dirt road home. I saw her once, sort of smiling, scolding herself about the wrapping job. About how she had to get it thick enough to hide the thing inside. She looked happy, but I knew it would be wrong for me to come out from the ditch where I lay hiding and watching ant colonies fight over a caterpillar in the red clay mud. I knew she did not want to be observed in this act. I don't know why. Things like that were never mentioned. As long as I knew her, they stayed wrapped. She was just like that — private, and cross when interrupted in herself.

The wrap around the book was to be respected too. I did not open it upstairs but carried it down to Aunt Maud. She would sigh and put down whatever she was reading.

I'd peel the tissue from the book and put the paper in the firebox beside the stove. She would then pick the book up off the floor, move to the couch by the window with me beside her but not touching, and begin to read.

Her voice came alive. Captain Hornblower novels, spies in King Arthur's court, stories of Egyptian kings and colour pictures of the dead inside their tombs of limestone. Whatever she could scrounge of the world from the town library came to vivid pulsing life in her deep, stern voice. I loved those readings, and the game of finding the book that began them.

I loved it when my Aunt Maud's sighs evaporated into the wind of all the world, specially for me.

We'd sit in the sun or behind the glass with the rain driving in off the bay. Reading and never touching, not even our arms. You did not touch Aunt Maud. Even The Aunts did not. She was the only person I ever saw them leave without a wrinkled kiss. When her visits were over they did not even lift their faces to receive her kiss. No one ever touched her. I don't know why. I never asked.

The Girls from Amherst

I saw them kiss. The Girls. On the lips and for a
long time. I was suddenly fascinated by them. They
were more than funny old ladies who gave me candy
and did my grandmother's hair in the olden days
before my father was born. The Girls had me over
for iced tea and let me pet their cat. Now they were
suddenly more — not what old ladies were
supposed to be. Not the same, not good the way old
ladies were. I didn't want this thing to be true but I
also hoped it was.

What else did they do?

I followed them. They were my prey. I owned
their deviance, they owed it to me. I looked for
aberrant behaviour everywhere, I watched them all

morning. I told Eli that I was observing them. I brought her reports of subtle glances and stolen caresses. She looked bored.

I took Claire information too but, watching Eli, she was worldly and pretended not to be surprised.

I finally took my stories to Mags, and she shrieked laughter about their antics into the wind until it was time for lunch.

In the afternoon Aunt Maud sat watching The Girls from Amherst come back from their walk, and I crouched behind their car pretending not to.

Uncle K had been helping The Girls' hired man with painting. I hovered around their cottage, out of sight. I was not supposed to be around when Duke was working. When he'd fixed the well box, I'd learned too many new words The Aunts found inappropriate. Besides, everybody in town knew not to let their daughters hang around old Duke Evans. Old grabber Duke, Eli called him. So I was spying carefully out of sight, behind the old brown Dodge The Girls brought to the shore on weekends. Spying on Lavinia and Margaret as they flopped along the beach under their straw hats, with their feet slapping the wet mud sand by the waterline.

Lavinia had the quiet of almost-tears this afternoon, and Margaret looked annoyed. They went inside their red cottage, past Uncle K painting the outside windowframes. They walked over Duke Evans, who was crouched underneath the porch reinforcing the floor supports, and the screen door slapped shut behind them. Duke slid out into the light and spat tobacco and words at Uncle K.

"So," he hawked, "do the old lizzies seem a little testy to you or is it just my eyes today?"

He said this in a loud voice, close to the door The Girls had just walked through. Too loud and too close. Uncle K walked away, after a pause, and then Duke spat in the grass again, laughed and rolled back under the porch.

I looked at the spit on the grass between the cottage and the Dodge. It glistened. Malice. Bright like blades or the broken shells that were smashed and left to dry in the sun by the boys on the mud flats. It glinted with the chrome on the mirrors of the car beside me. Inside the cottage I could hear The Girls fighting: loud sharp words and silences. Duke was listening too, and laughing under the boards.

I didn't want him listening to them, spying. He was dangerous, though, and not to be approached. I looked at the cottage and saw Margaret's face through the windows of her sunporch. She had an expression I could not pin down; it was not a look I'd seen before. I knew I had no right to be looking in, and I was immediately and inexplicably ashamed to see it, I didn't know what it meant but I knew it was not supposed to be seen by anyone — not by old Duke Evans, not by me. I ran back to our cottage, keeping the car between me and the shine of the spit-covered grass.

I can't always easily get away from what I start.

Margaret came to smoke beside my Aunt Maud on our veranda in the last of the afternoon sun. She smiled as I went past her. She did not see that she had been betrayed.

"God-damned annoying," I could hear her saying. I tried not to listen but she kept talking. Aunt Maud has people who come to visit her and tell her everything about their lives. They talk without interruption, without taking a breath, without need of her response. They talk to Maud and then they wander off until they need to talk to her again.

Margaret talked to Aunt Maud about the fight she and Lavinia had had that afternoon. She said the kinds of things I'd been listening for, but I didn't want to know them now.

I kept remembering the look — the one I had stolen earlier in the day — and Duke spitting at them on the grass. I was stealing now, listening out of sight, but I didn't want to be. I hoped that someone would find me there inside the window, or that she would stop talking and go home. It didn't occur to me to make an active choice and go away myself. I was frozen by this person's metamorphosis from deviant to woman.

Eventually Margaret stopped talking, said goodbye and left our veranda. Aunt Maud called after her to come over any time she felt down, and then she sat back down to pet the cat until the evening wind came in.

She was, as usual, still and silent. Unflappable,

indestructible; conservative, unmoving and unshockable. How do some people have this quality that makes other people want to talk to them? Why do people want to tell her things, I wondered. She never hid behind cars to find things out about people, they just sat down beside her and, almost by accident, delivered up their secrets freely. I wondered if she ever felt ashamed, the way I did, about knowing so much so easily. When I asked her about this later; she told me she'd never been ashamed, but she'd often been afraid that people would hate her because they had given away too much.

Lamp

The power and phones were out and The Aunts had
come to walk up the beach with Maud. They were
going to check on the other cottages and to tell the
storm news. Uncle K was at the Mayfair marking
time for his turn to go out looking on the sea with
the other men; the Wilson boys had not come in
from the water yet, but close to shore the bay was
still ugly so the men were waiting. I was left to my
own devices.

It was an eerie night up at the top of the
cottage, Aunt Maud's regular breathing passing
through the storm. A strange, blue, crashing night.
When the rain stopped, its absence was a sound.
When the storm ended and I heard my Aunt

Maud's breathing, I finally slept. It was thick and foggy sleeping.

§

The driftwood stick I carried had washed up in the storm. Its end was rounded and fit into my hand. I whittled the other end with my jackknife. The point came out perfectly, not splitting or breaking off like real driftwood does. It stayed strong and sharp and true, as if it were carved from bone.

Seaweed covered the sand in front of the cottage, thrown there by the storm. It was a thick black net stretching from the point to the fort. In it were bits of what the storm had hurled at the shore. Scraps of pottery and the twitching skins of storm-beached fish glinted in the bright noon sun.

I walked to the shore creek. Well, pushed my way through the wet, stinking seaweed. I'd never seen it like this. It usually just marked the high-water point, and showed the places where the winter storms had come. I'd looked at it before and not believed that the sea would ever wash so high. Now the seaweed was here in summer, and up to my thighs. It was thick and wet; I was used to it being wispy, and silver where the salt dried in it. My legs sank down into it and my feet were swallowed in scratchy muck. It was entrapping, like the quicksand in the Tarzan movies. When I poked it with my driftwood stick, it sprang back. It was alive, and evil.

I always went to the creek after storms. It was then that the muck twisted up the bleached bones of cattle. I was drawn to the purity of bone. I did not connect these sea-bleached skulls with the death of any real thing. I wanted to show them to Mags and Claire — the bones of dinosaurs bleached clean by the ocean salt.

Just before the shore creek, the seaweed was at its thickest. It had pulled itself into a heavy black hill that I could see just after I left the cottage. I moved closer and the black hill began to define itself. I slowed my progress. As the shape grew clear and real, I moved as slowly as I could. When I was close enough to touch the hill, I stopped.

A smooth, glossy shape thrust out of the weed in front of me. A chestnut body linked the seaweed and the bank. The thinly covered spine bones of a fallen horse became clear, black grass curling up around the flanks. The great barrel of side and belly rested in the mud of the creek. The crest and neck and the quiet ears had been tossed onto the sand that crept up from the rocks to the pasture beside the shore creek. The sand around the head was beginning to dry, turning golden in the sun. The soft blond sand was not moving at all. When you looked at it closely, you could always see it swirling over the surface of the beach, but today even the lightest sand was quiet. The great soft mane was still in the sun and the quiet day. I think that is the only absence of wind I ever remember at the shore.

I moved around the horse, slowly, towards its face. I don't know what I expected; open eyes, I suppose. Dead or alive, I thought its eyes would be open. When people died on TV, someone always had to close their eyes with a kind hand. They had to touch the dead person and shake their heads saying, "No," or "There's nothing we can do now." That was the way things died. With people making announcements. With commotion and sound and activity.

I pushed through the seaweed and came around to the creature's face. It was quiet and the eyes were not open. A scattering of sand and seaweed had swept up over the silver hairs on the muzzle. I waited for drama. Waited for breath. Movement. None came.

I looked at the huge feet flung brokenly through the seaweed. The face rested without the twitching lips of the sleeping horses I had known. I stood with my driftwood stick on the windless beach and watched.

When I finally moved, I did something that I still don't understand. I scraped and pulled every bit of seaweed away from the horse. At first I used my stick, and then I had to grab great bundles of the stuff and pull it away. It was important to free the chestnut skin from the black weed. It was necessary to free it to the sun and to let the sand around turn gold again. I worked at it all afternoon.

The last things to wipe away were the sand and strings of black seagrass on her face. The horse had become specific to me by the end of my work. She had become real as her death opened up to the afternoon and then to the evening.

The mare's skin was warm from the sun, I think, when I finally reached out to touch her face. The seaweed and the sand pushed easily away from the silver muzzle. I picked up my stick and walked along the rocks at the top of the bank. As I walked away from the bones of the shore creek, the light of the day was ended and the wind had come in off the sea.

§

Aunt Maud's feet were cold. I could feel the cold from them in the orange blankets beside my own. Even sleeping I didn't touch Aunt Maud. When I was afraid, though, caught in the blue of a storm-night dream, there was no one warmer and stronger to keep the dark away. She could sleep with the light on, and on nights when she thought I might be afraid she would leave it lit. I could always find my way to her in storm nights. She understood everything about dignity, and never mentioned my creeping in beside her to anyone.

III University Visits

Coffee, First Cup

The coffee is still hot. Tin taste of instant, but hot. James leans against the corner veranda post and watches me. He wants to know about me, about who else has been here with me. I tell him.

Normally I would find this question too possessive, strange, dangerous. But there is an advantage here. I don't know him well enough not to tell him everything. I'm also no longer interested in the game of pretending to have no past.

Sophomoric

In university, I took a man to town to see The
Aunts. They gave him my Uncle Edward's special
anniversary cup. I got Aunt Maud's blue one. This
meant that I was thought of as a little odd, strange,
a loose cannon, while the man was being given the
chance to equal the mythic Uncle Edward. MLA,
you know, lovely man. Successful. Married to Aunt
Byrd for forty-seven years.

The cup they gave my "man friend" was
special. That was what they called him: "Your man
friend" or "your young man". "Gentleman caller"
was vulgar and American. That cup had come to
Aunt Byrd on what would have been her golden
anniversary. Death was no obstacle to marriage in
my family.

Cups for tea were carefully selected. One could come up to meet the expectations of a proper cup given the chance. They always put out the test of the cups with proper china smiles.

The man was blind to the honour, but he blundered into their good graces for ever when he smiled and told them it was an elegant and lovely pleasure to drink tea in the way it was intended — in the company of lovely ladies in such a lovely home. He smiled at them and flirted about the Liberal government. They loved him, but he made a fatal error with me. He was nice. He was charming. And he was, as my Aunt Maud said after I dumped him, as phony as a three-dollar bill. He brought to the surface an immediate and irrational urge in me to shock him, to shock The Aunts. To make them revolve in their graves.

The Aunts had been interred at birth. They could revolve in their graves long before they attained them. I saw them do it.

I have always thought of this revolving, not as an elegant turning, but as a series of quickening revolutions. Faster and faster, around and around. Like a rotisserie on a barbecue gone mad. Whiz, whirl, spin, spin, spin.

The Aunts revolved in their graves about any number of things. The afternoon of the visit with my young man they revolved when I told them that the fable of the little red hen was from the Bible. Well, it seemed like a Bible story to me. It was about someone who knew something that the others didn't know and got the upper hand because of it.

So this little red hen is making bread while the lazy animals rest in the sunshine. When winter comes and the bread is made, the little red hen lives and the other animals all die. The little red hen says something snaky like "Well, while I laboured you dwelt in idleness and I will have no one labour to help me eat my bread," so this bitchy little hen goes into her coop while the other animals die by heating vents, under newspapers, in the street. I bet she even sleeps well. She votes PC and firmly believes that all people have a choice. She has no idea that she's lucky.

I tended to think that the Bible was written to make you feel afraid of being bad because you might miss out on something. The thing was, though, I was sure it was the good people who were missing out on something. Good people like The Aunts. Held to codes of behaviour by who they were, by the horizons of the town their father had built and by the Bible stories they had been told as children.

The Bible and little red hen connection escaped The Aunts. Stupidly, arrogantly, not recognizing that their silence was that of shock and not of interest, I continued to explain: the little red hen parable was clearly similar to the Bible story about the virgins and the lamp oil.

Well, these smart virgins save their lamp oil and sit around in the dark all night while the dumb virgins play cards and talk about their life expectations over coffee. When the bridegroom comes to take them to the party, only the smart virgins can go. The dumb ones had a nice female bonding experience all night and ran out of oil. The snitty little smart virgins won't share their lamp oil, so the good-time virgins don't get to go to the party or the dance or whatever. I can't figure that the good-time virgins would be real interested in going to a party with a bunch of so-called intelligent virgins who are prepared to sit around in the dark all night waiting for some man to come and get them. All in all, I think the dumb virgins were better off.

And what about that poor guy who builds his house on the wrong foundation? Love Canal ring a bell? PCBs? How are you supposed to know?

I mean, really, don't you see what kind of messages the Bible stories are sending? I mean, beyond the text, there's a clear message, right? And I won't even start about the misogyny. It's the biggest piece of anti-woman literature ever written, and we use it as an authorized guidebook!

Well, after I stopped, The Aunts and the man just kind of smiled. They all got that glazed look, and for a while nobody looked at anything but the tea service. Then The Aunts looked at my "man friend" and blinked. He smiled politely and dropped his chin back into my Uncle Edward's teacup.

The Aunts were crushed. They blinked and moved their Avon-tinted lips a little. Then, slowly, surely and methodically, holding their teacups on their saucers, they began to turn. I watched them whiz, whirl and spin, spin, spin. They spun in the tomb of their house, with its doily-covered armchairs and its banished dust. They looked at me and at the man, and they revolved together, faster and faster and faster, in their ever-living graves.

Graduate

Once, in November, I went to the shore.

§

I walked to the university pool. The place was
generally deserted in the evening, the sounds hollow.
The basketball games in the upstairs gyms had
finished. The athletes had walked their proud and
directed steps away from the games that set them
apart from the rest of us. The scorekeepers had
picked up their clipboards and all the mothers had
come by to pick up the last of the kids at Saturday
lessons.

The pool was open for another half-hour

when I went inside and crept downstairs. At the equipment counter a beautiful woman with a long blonde braid stood talking to a man. She leaned into the counter he stood behind. They wore sweat pants and worn team shirts. The woman stood jingling her keys while she smiled up at him.

I recognized them from a pamphlet the university had made. They were two of the beautiful people, the kind who entice parents to send their children to the ivy-covered, safe, brick places of education. They were unhurt by life or by anyone living in it around them.

The woman smiled and lifted her keys at me without stopping her talk. The man leaned out of the equipment room and smiled. "Pool closes in half an hour." The way he spoke was like the way she lifted her keys. It was done without thought or malice, it was done without interrupting the flow of conversation. The kind of speaking that only people who were never beaten down could share. This was the kind of conversation I had had, or had tried to look as though I was having, before last night in my dorm room when my ex-boyfriend had surprised me one more time with flowers and another card. The kind I was capable of yesterday, before I knew that even men you had loved before could hurt you with astonishing ease and then get up and dress and wander home again, leaving you to concentrate on breathing.

I looked at those two lovely people and hated them all the way down the stairs to the pool. I hated them for not seeing me and understanding that I had to swim all night. That was all I wanted to do, and now I only had half an hour to submerge my burning body.

I hated them for not knowing I was lost from their world; I would have hated them more for knowing. They were in another place. They were clean and pure and lucky.

I swam in the tepid chlorine water.

I swam lengths until I could not breathe at all, and then I swam two more.

The tiles in the shower room were steamy. A left-over shower was running at the far end. I peeled away my suit — "skin suits", Aunt Maud had called them, and all the girls had laughed. I pulled the skin down around my body and stepped out of it. I lay retching on the tiles until I caught my breath, and then I pulled on the shiny skin and went in again to swim.

It was not enough.

I needed to be in the water at the shore.

I borrowed a truck from a friend and pushed its resisting gears all the way to the cottage. I smoked cigarettes from the glove compartment and listened to music, and screamed along with all the songs on the tape. I'm not sure what the music was, but the cigarettes were menthol. I stopped at an Irving store and ordered coffee, but I left before the Irving girl had even gone to find a cup for me to take away. I had the heat on and the windows down. My shoulders hurt. I burned myself twice with matches before I remembered that trucks sometimes have lighters. I have no idea how fast I drove.

The cottage was an hour away from school. I'd stolen the keys from Aunt Maud and copied them last summer. I let myself in to the complete dark of the place. The shutters were on and the power had been turned off for the winter. I lit a fire in the Franklin stove and took off my clothes in the blue light from the burning driftwood fire.

I went outside and down to the water. When I could see the lighthouse from around the turn in the beach, I began to swim.

After I'd pulled my body through the water as far as the shore creek, my legs began to cramp. Then my arms and shoulders, then my neck and stomach. After only a little more I began to sink. It felt so much better than trying to move.

My face dragged along the sand, and I let the waves tug at my body. I felt the way I've often felt the instant before sleep. The salt taste had left my mouth, or left the part of me that cared. The whole world was above me in thick black water. Things floated out of the world and into the spaces behind my eyes.

Fishermen don't learn to swim when they fish this water. Most of them say they'd be dead from the cold in about five minutes anyway. I thought of this — of belonging with the men I'd seen with Uncle K at the tavern. Square-hewn fingers around brown bottles. Hands smoking. Working hands. Hands holding and tearing.

No. Think of belonging. It was nice to belong with such people. Strong people, people who lived through starvation and spat out at the government.

How nice to just relax and belong to something. Safety.

Belonging to something. The cottage. I'd left a fire burning before I walked into the sea. I must go in and stop it.

The logic in dreaming is simple. Cars become rooms, rooms become castles and castles become cars again. This is all right in dreams and in drifting into sleep. This is all right in any drifting.

My legs scraped bottom and my fingers were stiff from cold. I couldn't tell if they were even held together. When swimming, I remembered, I should always hold my fingers together to make a solid paddle. Women, girls at the YMCA who had taught me how to swim. What happened to them? Did they have to survive, or did they just live on for ever in their maple-leaf bathing suits, teaching smaller women to swim around in chlorine pools? I heard their advice. Remembered their clean, strong voices. "Fingers held together are more efficient. Might save yer life some day," the pretty girls at the Y had said, their voices echoing down to all the children bubbling in the water below them.

"Air in, water out," they said. "Might save yer life some day." I spat out water by lifting my head out of the November ocean, and began to breathe. I couldn't understand how I could breathe by simply lifting up my head. Wasn't it supposed to be more difficult?

My legs scraped across a rock, and the motion of the icy waves pushed at my right side. Sand prickled under my chin. My eyes ached with salt. I lay in shallow water where the incoming tide had washed me up. Safe.

I lay there in six inches of water thinking of the drowned men of November. I tried to cough but realized I hadn't taken in enough water. Some part of me laughed, and I pulled my body back up the beach and into the fire-lit cottage.

I took an afghan off one of the upstairs beds and brought enough wood in from the sunporch to keep me warm all night. I could sleep. I'd find my clothes in the morning. I pulled the afghan to the floor. It had been knit by my Aunt Maud and relegated to the sunporch for its violent orange colour. I pulled it close around me. I crept warm and soft into sleeping, with the fire strong beside me.

I began to drift away. Away from hands and bruises and from my own body on the floor of my room at school. I drifted away from eyes and away from the woman I had been yesterday. I organized my drifting. I drifted into the smell of the fire and the salt wood at the cottage. The drifting was easier after a night of drownings. The smell of the place was good. The wind outside moaned of being home. People were looking in on me. The people who belonged here. Always would, I thought.

I can stay here.

I remembered something from a course I had taken. Virginia Woolf walked into the water with stones in her pockets. She killed herself to stay at the shore for ever.

IV Uncle K

The Mayfair Tavern, Then and Now

The wind is up and the tents of my people are overcrowded with ghosts. Tents of my people, that's what my Dad calls the cottage. My mother calls it the clan hall. Whatever it is, it must be left for the moment. I put my lists into my pocket and walk in to town, to the Mayfair Tavern.

It is afternoon and James has gone back to sleep. I love anyone with the confidence to nap, but I've never been able to sleep for a short time without waking up feeling drugged. I'm also very hungry.

It seems easier to go by myself than to go inside and wake him. Besides, he's turning out to be the rare kind of person who's not threatened by my need to be alone.

I did read somewhere that sleeping people are never bothered by real spirits. Too much competition from their own living dreams. He will be fine among my family ghosts. I, however, need a rest from them.

The Mayfair, Then

When Uncle K visited The Aunts' house, he was not allowed to drink. At nine years of age, the idea of not being allowed to do things was not in the least odd. We were both childish and shared status as people who should know better but never did; it made us perfect accomplices. On the days during my first summer alone at the shore, when Uncle K couldn't get into the kitchen to slip rum into his tea, we'd go for walks. We went to the store to buy molasses cookies with jam in the centre.

That was my chosen role. Ally. The lines of this part were "We went to the store to buy molasses cookies. They were lovely cookies." We did actually go to the store. Every time, on the way home from the Mayfair Tavern, we stopped at the store, we bought cookies and we ate them on the road. Uncle K didn't want me lying to my family. As he was Presbyterian, the sin of omission did not particularly bother him.

The Mayfair Tavern was a big square room in a tall brick building that used to be a movie theatre. Movie *house* — it was a longer time ago than movie theatres. The tavern, "the tav", had a door at one end and a tall wooden bar at the other. The windows and the chipboard walls were painted black; it was illegal to have windows open to the street back when the tavern was created, and curtains were a bother. Light was diffused and came from bulbs on the end of thick black wires. When the bulbs swung in a breeze from the opening door, the place became a rocking ship. At other times the light was soft and still, smoke-filtered, the gentle light of a barn in winter. It was warm there.

There was always a slick of beer on the floor. I could feel my shoes stick slightly in the tack of it as I followed Uncle K inside. The bar surface itself was always clean, mopped with an ash-covered rag in the hand of the bartender.

The bartender was an understanding man. He always let us bring the bicycle in off the street. He looked away as Uncle K put his bulky roll of dollars in their elastic band back into his pocket. You didn't look at where another man kept his money, I learned. The bartender never looked. He also never charged for my Pepsi. I played songs on the jukebox and he smiled: "If You Want to Play in Texas, You've

Got to Have a Fiddle in the Band" and "Your Cheatin' Heart Will Tell on You".

I sat with my feet up on the barstool. I could swing it around as many times as I wanted to. I could kick at the rungs or tap my feet against the bar. Nobody ever told you to stop doing anything here. I could get two fat white straws for my Pepsi and stick them on my teeth for walrus imitations. This wasn't much good, though. Nobody told you to quit doing anything, but nobody noticed much either. Mostly, I sat beside my Uncle K while he drank two draft beer.

The people in the bar in the afternoons were like my Uncle K — tall, grey, quiet. They sat in the smoke and the beer and played cribbage until the evening, when most of them went home. They came up to the bar for cigarette change or for darts. "Quiet today, Kendal," they might say, or "Wind's up a bit." Most of them were listeners.

The bartender liked my Uncle K "What's the stupidest thing you ever did, K?" He wiped the rail with his cloth. I watched his hands. He had one shrunken arm — a baby's limb, pink and chubby — which he kept curled up against his chest. The other hand had long, dirty nails. Uncle K never looked at his arm, and the bartender didn't acknowledge my uncle's stutter. This was a relief. I hated the defending I had to do with many of the people in town.

"Well now. Stupid. I guess that would be the moose. Probably the moose. I was workin', then, out by Sussex Corners. I'd walked a fair bit into the woods with some of the boys from camp when we came upon a moose. Stuck. Stuck right between two skinny trees. Wedged. Couldn't move an inch and madder'n hell. I climbed up one of the trees, full of piss and vinegar, and sat myself right down on the neck of the bull. Well now, I guess that was motivation enough, for he got himself unstuck in short order. Broke both my fool legs. The boys had to fix up a rig with two popal poles and an overcoat and drag me two hours home over the snow. It was sort of clear that we'd all took a drink, and we lost both job and paycheque. Took me a whole winter with my sisters to heal over. I guess it was worth it. I don't know another man in town who ever rode a moose."

"Don't know that I know one now," the bartender said, winked at me and handed me a foil bag of salty peanuts over the bar. He teased Uncle K about the story as if it were a lie, as if he were any other man in town. "Tall stories," he said, and included us in the village.

My Uncle K would never let me lie. If the girls ask you directly, he said, you turn me in. If they don't ask, you say what you will. But don't you ever lie to anyone directly.

When we got back to the cottage The Aunts said, "How was the walk, dear?"

Uncle K never looked at me at these times. He usually walked away, out of sight and earshot. I could say whatever I felt I should. It was up to me. But I liked the tavern. I liked the smoke and the bar stool and the bartender's dirty nails.

"The walk was fine. We went to the store and got molasses cookies. They were very lovely cookies."

Coffee

I was fascinated by coffee. I wanted to drink it, but I was not allowed to. Uncle K felt that coffee was not the prerogative of fast women and businessmen, city people. He felt that I should be allowed to try some if I wanted to.

The Aunts did not think a nine-year-old girl in their charge for the day should be drinking anything their brother had around to offer. This was a running battle when we visited at Uncle K's.

He lived in a leaning dump of a brown house which a man from outside the town had given him instead of money for some job. It had a summer kitchen with back stairs that I was allowed to climb. I wasn't supposed to go into the room they led to, because there were holes in the rotting floor. I'd seen them in the ceiling of the room below.

There was also a hole in the floor of the summer kitchen for keeping things cool. It was filled with blue, mouldy bottles of pickled vegetables.

The walls of the room were completely covered with the kitchen equipment of my Uncle K. Pots, white enamel kettles chipped and covered in rust, milk bottles thick with dust. Every shelf above the reach of The Aunts on kitchen chairs was fuzzy with orange, rusty dust. Every shelf above Aunt-level was covered with paper, catalogues, lamps, lightbulbs, metal lumps, fox traps and bits of broken pottery. Most of the pottery was blue. He picked it up along the shore because it was the colour of eyes.

On the Aunt-level shelves there was evidence of battle. Clean, neatly ordered shelves were lined with wax-paper shelf liners, cookie tins with good fresh baking in them and clean, shining dishes.

The parlour was filled with furniture. We had to go in single file and sit among the dusty covers. My Uncle K had also taken furniture for work during the Depression. We sat there with The Aunts and visited.

Everyone in the room sat at a different height. The chairs were all from different times and stuffed to different thicknesses. The variety of clocks showed almost three o'clock, no matter what the time was. "They keep good time twice every day," Uncle K whispered when I asked him about the clocks. Dust was everywhere.

The Aunts sat straight on the horsehair sofa, their stiff backs to the window. I perched on a wooden bench with a back and arms; it had a scratchy brown cover that I had seen in one of the catalogues in the kitchen stacks. Aunt Maud sank into a decrepit ladies' chair placed beside my bench.

We sat and drank and visited.

When I think of us all sitting there in our unmatched chairs with the smell of dust and lamp oil around us, I think of the settings for dusty murder mysteries. Mystery, intrigue, suspense.

I also think of my first sips of coffee, snuck to me by Uncle K in a mug The Aunts believed was filled with tea.

The Stuttering School

Uncle K had gone to the stuttering school in
Boston. I was not clear on why someone might be
sent there. Aunt Wynd said he went after the war.
Because of the shock. She whispered this — "The
Shock." Shock treatment, I guessed and thought of
the school. There would be huge rows of wooden
desks with wired-up inkwells, and a schoolmaster
with some kind of electric shock device. He would
use this device, or the threat of it, to make his
students stutter. They had to go because they had
been in the war.

At school on Remembrance Day we saw films
about the war. Long lines of jerkily moving, grey
young men who fell through barbed wire onto the

ground all over Europe. Canadians had urinated on their handkerchiefs so they could stay in the mustard gas longer, the film voice said. Then the film showed us old men in grey coats standing at cenotaphs with blood-red roses in their shaking arms and then we saw them as young men again. We saw them crawling out of the ocean and up onto a long clear beach. On the beach above the high-water mark there were other men, with guns and different helmets. As the Canadians crawled out of the sea, these other young men shot them.

The film broke; the voice was shaky, underwater-sounding. The teacher fixed it and then the camera looked up and down the clear and open beach at all the dead young men. The grey water pulled some of the bodies back into the sea. Others were tickled by the edge of the water. I could tell that the tide was coming in, and that after the film stopped all the bodies would be pulled into the sea.

I wondered if any of the bodies could wash up at Indian Point. I imagined them floating beneath the top layer of water. They might brush against your foot. They were seaweed, trapped between the sand and the air, tousled by the moving water. They might brush their stiffened fingers lightly against your leg as the waves rolled their bodies around in the sea.

July was the warmest time, but it was the time of jellyfish and sand-clouded water, and for me it was the time of bodies underneath the surface. Not just the drowned soldiers, but all the others who had been buried at sea, or abandoned there. I kept peering through the murk for Nelson, Henry Hudson, the fishermen in the Point Escuminac disaster, the extras in the Errol Flynn movies, and all the ordinary men who walked into the sea. But the thing that started my horror of July swimming was the soldiers in the films at school.

When I asked Uncle K about the war, he said it was all pretty dull until you got shot. That's all he'd ever say. He could never be made to talk about the war, not by me, not by The Aunts.

I wondered if this refusal to talk to The Aunts was why he might have been sent to the stuttering school in Boston.

The Mayfair, Now

Places don't change much when there's no money. The cribbage players are still here, although they seem much younger to me now. The smoke is the same, some of it probably exactly the same. I'm not sure the doors have ever been opened wider than the shoulders of the tall, grey drinking men. The floor is scuffed and tacky with beer. There's music — Hank Williams, Willie Nelson, Rita MacNeil. My friends in theatre find my taste in country music anachronistic. They expect me to like Kd. lang. They don't know that Patsy Cline existed and did her own songs once. The music here is real and comforting. The draft is cheap and the bar is solid.

Walking in this time I have no guide, but I

feel at home here. The one thing that's different is that now people look at me as I wander in. They see a stranger, despite my feelings of familiarity. The bartender watches me. His arm is smaller than I remember it. I sit on the stool at the bar and smoke. Comfortable as I am here, no one knows who I am. The bartender tells me they don't get many visitors; I know he means women. He's not being nasty or challenging, just informative. I used to come here as a kid, I tell him. He tells me that's impossible as he's never served minors, and then he winks. No, I mean as a little girl. He looks at me for a moment and smiles. I wouldn't have known you at all, he says.

We talk for a while, and he brings me two draft beer and a bag of peanuts. I learned as a kid that you always order two, put salt in them and then give over whatever change is left from the bill. You put it on the bar or on the tray; you don't give money, as if it were a favour, into someone's hands. He looks away as I put my wallet in my purse.

He tells me that my Uncle K was a fine man and he's missed. I like this. I'm not sure there is another place in town where it would be said. I smoke for a while and drink the salty beer as the men play cribbage and the bartender wipes the bar and then the tables. It's quiet and soft here, out of the wind. It is not, however, a break from memory. I tell the bartender thanks, and he lifts his ash rag at me as I leave the dusty tavern.

The road back is strange. The road is dry in September, red and packed hard from the summer travellers. I'm feeling lost, wrong somehow. Then I remember.

There are teenagers on the steps of the store. They watch me silently; strangers at this time of year always draw attention. I leave money on the counter with a young girl I don't know, and carry a brown paper bag outside. Inside are three molasses cookies which I eat as I walk the road home to Indian Point.

V The Aunts

Midafternoon

James has noticed some of their things on the
shelves here. He has noticed that The Aunts are
different in every story. He wants to know why. He
wants to know what I remember most about them.

I give him the foil bag of peanuts I brought
back from the tavern, and while he eats them I
consider his question. When he is finished I have
decided what I remember. Poise.

My Aunts were poised. At all times and in all
places. In every situation, they were poised.

Bread and Wynd

Aunt Wynd was making bread today, because Aunt Byrd did not trust the bakery in town for anything important. This bread was important because we were baking it for the Saint Pauls Annual Poor Boys' Picnic. Proceeds would go to charity. To the local poor families, said Aunt Wynd, and she smiled. I knew I was dead if Eli or her cousins caught me anywhere near this Poor Boys' Picnic. I decided to have the flu tomorrow, but today I watched Aunt Wynd making the bread.

The bread dough thwacked against the side of the blue enamel bowl. We had to use the blue one because the brown earthenware one was too small for the bread to rise. The measuring cup was the blue tin one in the fourth canister on the third shelf of the pantry. Everything had its place in The Aunts' white kitchen. The table, the windowseat with its sea-green cushions and the cupboards along the back kitchen wall — each had its own position. I sat at the table watching Aunt Wynd's back push against her dress as she played with the dough. It was almost ready to rise again.

Aunt Byrd had visitors on the porch most of the morning, so Aunt Wynd and I were left alone in the kitchen.

Bread has to rise twice, not counting the yeast. It has to be kneaded and thumped and switched from bowl to bowl to loaf pans. It has to be shaped and coaxed and prodded. It has to be created.

It takes all afternoon.

By the time it actually got to go in the oven I was ravenous. By the time it began to smell like bread I was desperate. Aunt Wynd sat with me at the table and tried to show me how the hands of bridge worked. Rubbers and tricks.

It took concentration to follow Aunt Wynd's mind across the cards. The bread smell was thick and wonderful as it swirled out of the oven and into the sunny kitchen. I wanted to take it out to devour it but Aunt Wynd said we had to wait for the expert. We had to wait for the one person in town who was known for always taking her loaves out at the perfect time. We waited.

Aunt Byrd finally came in to check our bread. Aunt Wynd got up and fluttered around her sister. She'd wanted to check it ten minutes ago, she said.

"Wynd, dear, you know you always take it out too early." Aunt Byrd moved decisively, precisely. She pulled the pans out and thumped them underneath twice with the heel of her oven-mitted hand. She flipped them out of their pans with one clean jolt and left them to cool on two clean bread racks. She smiled at us, told me to lead with trump and went back to her guests on the porch. I waited for Aunt Wynd to stick out her tongue. I always did when anyone came into what I was doing and took it over. It always led to trouble, because I left my tongue stuck out until it insulted someone. I waited. Nothing.

"Don't you mind being bossed?"

"Oh, no, dear. I'm not being bossed. Your Aunt Byrd just likes to keep us organized. She had the devil of a time with Father, as he was just the same way. We all have to find our own way in a family, my dear. You have Father's eyes, you know." She looked at me for a moment with her washy blue expression and nodded. I knew she was not seeing me. "I learned to step around their arguments and keep myself content. Your Aunt Maud steps around us by making her world in books. K — well, he's never really been what he might have been, but he's been himself. I am simply quiet. Don't ever mistake a quiet room for a still one. Now, you put down the spade, dear. Lead with trump."

I did, and she took it and smiled. She won all the tricks and then showed me how I might have played my hand. She smiled and drank her tea and never raised her voice above a whisper. I watched her win the cards and place them down with her fluttery hands all afternoon.

We ate some of the fresh, warm bread with butter my Uncle K had got for work at Nasons' farm. We drank our stove-boiled tea and listened to the voices organize the picnic out on the porch.

The next day Aunt Maud told The Aunts I had a horrible stomach-ache, probably flu. But Aunt Byrd decided that it was the bread. Aunt Wynd had made it with bad eggs Uncle K had brought, she said, so it was put out for the birds. Neither me nor the bread made it to the picnic. The Aunts took cookies and a new white Ladies' Bible for the church auction instead. I spent the whole day in bed, trying to figure out the way my aunt had been playing her cards the day before.

It wasn't until I learned to play bridge myself that I realized she cheated. The rules of the strange game she played that afternoon were designed for her to win. It wasn't until they had been gone from the house in town for years that I really thought about her quiet cheating. I have finally decided that I don't resent it. I admire it. She was right. We all have to find our own way in a family. She was also right about stillness in a room; I learned from her never to mistake a quiet room for a still one. I miss her kind of quietness, and so, whenever I play at cards, I cheat.

No one will ever play with me for money. "Card shark," they say.

"Yes," I say, "I have my Aunt Wynd's hidden teeth."

Byrd Song

The great upstairs of the house on Main Street
became known to me only after Aunt Byrd retired
grandly, in the tradition of my family, to expire.
When she ascended to the second floor she took a
police-band radio with her. This monitor of violence
terrified me. I can't even watch the news. She gloried
in it.

The radio became her network, a complement
to the one she had with the women of the town. She
sat among her pillows with the static calls and voices
pounding across the rigid order of the room. She
required her visitors to shout over the radio. She
refused to turn it down, let alone off.

My Aunt Byrd thoroughly enjoyed being

difficult. She had all her women-friends climb the broad, winding staircase to her room. She received visitors twice weekly. She had a polished silver tray for cards. She withdrew entirely from men; she said it was not seemly for them to be upstairs while she was in her bed.

This modesty was actually orchestrated to prevent the minister from coming to her spiritual aid. His theology was unsound, she said. His nose was indecently large. She simply did not trust the man. She accused him of trying to take her silver tray out in his pants. She compared him to Judas and told him he would have no chance to betray her. Certainly he would have no more chances at her silver.

Aunt Maud explained all this to me later. It seems he had preached to Aunt Byrd from a passage of the Bible that indicated to him that women should not speak — that they should be obedient and kind, never wilful or proud. He alone was enough to make Aunt Byrd believe in ordaining women. He was never received again. Not in her room, and not in her house.

In her room the bed was iron and white. The curtains were muslin and white. Aunt Byrd amid her pillows was pale and clean and white. The strong white of ironed flannel sheets, blinding and unpredictable snowstorms and leaping ocean foam. Everything was clean, pure and elegant.

We would sit there in the pale room with the breeze blowing in and speak above the police-band radio. This struck me as morbid, this line of polite chatter above the calls of beatings, drunkenness and stolen trucks. You were supposed to chat while the world erupted into chaos all around you.

I shouted remarks about my job, or sanitized versions of my daily life, over the static and the voices. Now I wouldn't leave out the apartment I shared with a boyfriend at the time, but then I thought it was important to spare her such things. She could have given me sound advice. She would have made him pay the rent, no matter how talented a musician he had the potential to be, but I'd been raised to protect the old and never asked.

She told me often not to shout, she was not deaf yet. She also thought that being critical of my employer was unbecoming. She did not appreciate what I thought were amusing and appropriate anecdotes. She couldn't stand to be patronized, but I didn't know another way to speak to her.

I was told not to upset Aunt Byrd. She upset me instead. She remembered every bit of trouble she had ever found me in. She told me about all the local crimes. Maybe she was linking these things, or maybe her mind was wandering. She digressed and mixed her thoughts. She spoke strangely enough to be interpreted as senile. But maybe she always had. When old women are confused and hard to follow, we assume senility. I think I should keep a journal as proof that my mind has always wandered. I'll pull it out when someone accuses me of becoming old, when someone sitting in my room some day begins to listen far too carefully to the way I speak.

The incongruity of not upsetting this elegant

old woman who knew the name of every busted drug dealer, every battered woman, was immense. I had my orders, though. No one wanted to disturb her peace.

One afternoon when I visited, no one told her that the latest housekeeper had quit. Aunt Wynd had gone to town to visit the doctor, and Aunt Maud was at the shore. I'd been left in charge. No one had told either one of us about my Uncle K's latest eccentricity.

Uncle K had gotten into the habit of removing his clothing on the doorstep of The Aunts' summer kitchen whenever he saw that it was empty. He liked to undress and then sit on the steps, wiggling his naked toes and smiling at the sky. It would have been handy to know this earlier than I did.

The radio buzzed in the white room.

Kch...kch...we gotta fight over at Whittakers', you wanna send Johnny out...kch...kch...

Aunt Byrd shouted at me for more tea and I poured it. "People do not know how to behave these days", she shook her head at the radio.

"No?"

I wondered if we needed more milk for the tea.

Kch...kch...we got another occurrence too, over at Main, just called in...kch...kch...

"That is entirely too close, my dear. This used to be a fine old neighbourhood. Pull this pillow a touch." I adjusted the pillow and asked her whether it was milk first or tea. I could never remember.

Kch...kch...you wanna boot it over to Main there

Johnny, before Whittakers', we gotta second call in...kch...kch...

Through the window I could see the town's faithful RCMP cruiser approaching the house. Our house. The tall white house of The Aunts, where my Uncle K was taking off his clothes and rolling on the carefully sculpted lawn. I could just see him from the corner of the window, rolling and smiling on the summer grass. I envied his freedom, but I had to do something to distract Aunt Byrd.

I began fussing around the room. I pushed her pillows, pulled at her jacket.

The radio chirped static, the RCMP officer smiled at K and moved towards him. Uncle K giggled and went rolling out of sight across the lawn.

The radio repeated the address and more static, and I wondered if my Uncle K had his own code number now. The door of the car was open and the radio was loud. The radio in Aunt Byrd's room was echoing its phrases exactly. My Uncle K was being arrested in stereo, right underneath Aunt Byrd's white, lace-trimmed curtains.

I began to natter about anything I could think of. I was watching hockey now. How was Aunt Wynd's hip? Had she heard there was a flu around? The code numbers bounced between the radios, and I chatted at full volume until the officer escorted a smiling Uncle K back into his clothes and then into the car. The door slapped shut. The voices stopped and the static ended. There was absolutely no reaction from Aunt Byrd. She hadn't heard, then.

My shouting over the radio and fussing over her bed jacket had worked. I released my breath. She smiled.

"No use in worrying, my dear. He does this every time the kitchen's empty. They will take him home and shortly they will call Aunt Wynd. She will hire a new girl from somewhere and will tell you not to upset me. She doesn't think I'm quite able to hear my radio, you see. She will see to it that life is at its best for me, and I will give your Uncle K his temperance scolding when he sobers up. Now sit down, stop chattering and hold that pale blue yarn while I gather it up. Then you can go down and get my tea. Mind you heat the pot, and it's the milk that goes in first."

§

Aunt Byrd continued to be in charge during the eleven years she spent upstairs. Her will was law. She controlled the money of her family and the title of her home. She was catered to between the bursts of static on her radio.

I hope that, when the time arrives, I will have inherited her steely elegance, her silver madness. Her poise and her stiff-held confidence.

I will not want the radio.

VI Perspective

James

I met him in the theatre where he works. I talked to him over coffee after dropping off my résumé with the production stage manager and the artistic director. He asked me where I'd done my apprenticeship and how I liked stage management and then really listened to my answer. He didn't roll his eyes when I told him I wanted to direct some day and he asked me what I liked about the show for which I was applying. No one asks stage managers what they like, they ask about experiences and skills but never about passions. Startled by him, I told him this and he said it was the accuracy with simultaneously running stop-watches that made us appear to be without desire. I laughed and he asked me again about the show and then put down his tape measure and really listened. The main woman character is a lot like Eli, she swore like a sailor and talked all the time. She even put Claire to shame. Funny, I still measure myself against a skinny twelve-year-old.

His hands were large. They dwarfed his coffee cup. "James" in blue was written on the side. I told him that his name was on a grave I knew at Indian Point. He said that was a very strange thing to tell someone. Well, it's a strange place, I guess.

While we were talking about the fort and Indian Point, the production stage manager says that they just received a fax from a stage manager whom they've been wanting to use for a while and thanks anyway for my interest. James said he was sorry, and I saw he meant it. He was nice, sympathetic, comfortable.

§

James was in my borrowed car, and we were on the road to the shore.

I couldn't decide if this was freedom or stupidity, but then it's not strangers you need to be afraid of. It's the people you know. I told him this, and then he fell asleep in the gently rocking car.

Near the border of New Brunswick, along the Sackville marsh where I went to school, he woke up and we went into the Irving for a burger. He drank milk with his food, tea after. He smiled a lot, a gentle smile. His hands reduced this cup too, as he

held it between the table and his mouth while he
spoke. He'd forgotten it was there, he was so
wrapped up in talking to me. He was glad to be
invited. He wanted to see the shore again. He
missed home from time to time, missed the wind.
Home for him is Nova Scotia, South Shore.

In the dark, back on the highway and then on
the earth road to the cottage, I told him all about
the Point. My family, the old hotel, the woollen
mill. In the dark he couldn't see that the mill was
condemned, the houses were unpainted. He couldn't
see the ragged wooden butterfly decorations on the
doors, the satellite dishes and the big dogs sleeping.
He didn't see the government lighthouse, metal and
unmanned since the Whittakers burned the old one.
He couldn't see any of it in the dark, but he was
from a place like this one; he would know.

§

At the cottage I stepped over the threshold, the one
that used to be there when I was small enough to
have to step over it. It had been gone for years, but I
only noticed its absence now. It's hard to keep track.
He watched me step over the air, watched me walk
around tables that had been gone for summers past,
remembering. He watched me look for the
matchbox where he couldn't see a shelf. He watched
my body remember.

More Visits

The Girls from Amherst had been walking the
beach. I'm sure they heard the car pull in last night
and wondered who was visiting at such an hour. I'm
sure Lavinia wondered who was so late getting out
of bed on such a lovely morning. They held off their
visit until late afternoon. I was impressed by their
restraint. I would have given in much earlier.

Margaret and Lavinia are hairdressers — were.
They were part of bridge parties, part of sandwiches
and tea and afternoons with The Aunts. They rented
a place just down the shore; we could see their red,
rented cottage from our veranda. They were summer
people. My grandmother used to have her hair done
at their cottage. They were invited to our cottage for

bridge and tea despite this fact. The Aunts were always gracious to the other classes.

After The Aunts got too old to make the walk out to the shore, The Girls kept an eye on the place. One eye — a concentrated force. They had watched The Aunts when they were alive, and now they watched the cottage. They watched and they wanted to know things. This afternoon they wanted to know who was visiting at the shore.

It was me, me and a man. A man who was here for the weekend because I liked his hands. He was here to be observed. He was here to pass tests he didn't know about. Tests I didn't know about.

This man-visit was an event in the life of the shore. The Girls did not take long to cross the sand and the unmowed grass to our veranda.

Margaret came to tea. Actually, she came *with* tea — in her canvas army surplus bag. She had been a WAC, and everything about her was canvas. Lavinia came with her. Floated with her — breezed, maybe — whatever describes the kind of footless wafting that carried her from place to place. She drifted. She trailed scarves. She moved in liquid chiffon flutters. She gardened, painted huge, sinister red and mauve-yellow roses and played the church hall piano whenever she could. She smiled at me from behind a passing chiffon flutter. Somehow she always looked as if she were being filmed through a filter for an ancient, delicate movie. She told me music had always been her first love, and blinked. Huge blue eyes blinked slowly in the sun.

Margaret laughed, cracking the filtered air,

and told me her Chopin sounded like pudding.

Margaret had become more frank. She had never been a tolerant woman. She had been one of the last visitors of my Aunt Byrd in her later days. Margaret was brash and warm and strong. She and Byrd had liked each other well, she said.

When she brought tea she also brought scotch. Lavinia sat with us and pulled lemon out of a flimsy scarlet beachbag. She fanned herself with a new straw hat while Margaret pulled her khaki baseball cap down around her eyes to hide them from the sun. Margaret freckled, Lavinia paled from heat exhaustion.

Lavinia was a southern belle from Moncton, New Brunswick. Margaret never mentioned a home. Lavinia said she had once served tea to visiting royalty. Margaret added that Lavinia was the famous New Brunswick waitress. The one who was heard by everyone present to say, "Keep your fork, Duke. There's pie coming."

Lavinia said that this was nonsense and that Margaret had grown especially spiteful in her declining years.

They sat there in the last of the afternoon sun, waiting for whomever I'd brought to come outside and be seen by them. They didn't ask. He didn't come out. The stalemate continued until the tea was gone. After that they wandered up the beach again in search of other events. It was an end-of-season afternoon, and most of the renters had gone home.

The Girls were bored.

Inside, James was trying to fit their retreating

backs into the people I'd told him about. He watched them moving down towards the darkening sand, holding each other's hands and walking their old and careful steps.

"I give up, which ones are they?"

"They are The Girls from Amherst, I'm surprised you couldn't pick them out. I told you about them before."

"You told me about them, all right." His arm was comfortable around my waist as we watched the beach hats retreat towards the lights beginning to blink into the evening from the other cottages along the shore. "But those little old ladies are most definitely not girls."

We lit a fire in the Franklin stove and curled up to eat the sandwiches he had picked up sometime during the day, while I was making lists.

VII Leave-Takings

Leaving

Sundays are for leaving. I hate leaving the cottage.
Aunt Maud said war gave romance to parting.
Leavings were romantic — a trifle final, perhaps,
but romantic all the same.

I could have lived in a time of war.

At this point I'm wondering what I've done.
I'm not sure this is a place for strangers. I have my
lists ready, but what if he is one of those people who
need logic in their packing? What if he thinks I'm
strange for taking things? I'm taking Aunt Maud's
slippers and the Monopoly board. I don't care what
he thinks.

Well, actually I do. That is the problem. This

man is no longer a stranger. He can reject this place, he can reject me and he can do it with full and complete knowledge. Strangers can't hurt you because they don't have all the facts. It's people who know you that you have to watch. They sneak up on you. When you least expect it, expect it.

What if he doesn't want to help carry the pump? It's my job now to take it to the city. I have it on my list.

I hate leaving here. It makes me nine years old. I want to take all my things with me. I want him to take something away with him; I hate not knowing if he will. I hate a number of things right now. I hate outsiders who have been let in, I hate being given title. Aunt Maud said never use the word "hate" unless you mean it. Save it. Use "dislike".

I dislike having to act grownup at the shore. I dislike sharing. I dislike difficult tasks. I dislike putting the toys away. I do not play well with others. I want it all my way.

I hate leaving.

Will he even know exactly where he's been?

Leaving, with Family

The cranes were out on the mud flats, and the wind was up. For the wind and the sea this was no different from any other Sunday in the last of August. It was different only for me. My family was coming to get me, coming to take me back to the city. It felt so strange to be nervous about seeing my own family. Aunt Maud was nervous too. She was moving around the cottage, checking on things. She dusted. I'd never seen her dust before; I thought the world around her just stayed neat. She straightened books on the shelves by the Franklin. She neatened the war-surplus bag with the kindling in it. She moved the bread The Aunts had made in and out of its brown paper bag, as if she were ready to cut it up for sandwiches, and then put it away again. My parents were bringing the baby and they were staying for lunch.

The baby. Now it was a real thing, but I hadn't even seen it. Uncle K said it would look like everyone in the room when The Aunts were finished with it. The Aunts would say it had my chin, Maud's eyes, their great-aunt Sarah's nose. He didn't expect to be given a body part by The Aunts. They were coming too, to see the baby. My brother, that was who this baby was. My brother.

I had always wanted an older brother. I'd thought of twelve as a good age for him. This one wasn't twelve, and when he was he still wouldn't be older.

I didn't want to be an older sister. Older sisters were neat in their own way, with their Partridge Family records and their lipstick, but they didn't ever want to play with younger sisters or their friends. When Claire's older sister played with us, she called it babysitting. We made fun of her boyfriend and her make-up, and we tried on all her clothes whenever Claire could sneak them out.

Being an older sister let you in for ridicule. Older sisters were mean and older and taller and they fought with everyone. I didn't want this baby to make me into one, but no one had asked me.

My father was better. He'd been so for two weeks, but they'd left me here while my mother got over having this baby. Babies made you sick, then. Why would anyone want one?

When they came in, my father was holding it. His arms were pale and his red freckles stood out. His beard had bits of grey in the red now, and he looked thin. My mother was enormous. Her stomach was round — not as much as when she was pregnant, but still big. I hadn't known she would still have a big shape. Now she was also someone else's mother. I loved her too much to share her with anyone. I hadn't known that until today. We all stood and looked at each other.

Uncle K coughed. Aunt Maud brought them inside. The Aunts came out of the porch and the cottage was suddenly moving again. My father smiled and brought the baby to me. My mother showed me how to hold his head, and told me that he needed support. My support. He needed me. The circle of the family started talking again, and on its edge I held the baby.

Soon it would be time to get into the car and drive away, but now, right now, I held my new brother and watched his eyes move around the room filled with his family. I wondered if he wanted a big sister or if he could understand that next week I'd be ten and we'd be back at home. I wondered if he could smell tobacco on Uncle K or Ivory on Maud or White Shoulders on The Aunts. I wondered what he thought of all of us. What he saw on his first time here at Indian Point.

What would he take away with him?

Leaving, as Duenna

James has helped with the shutting up. He's done
what I asked without questioning the method. He's
followed my lists and ignored my spelling. He's
helped out with all the illogical closing rituals of the
cottage.

> —Dishes upstairs under the bed in the back
> bedroom.
> —Pump in the car.
> —Stovepipe inside the sunporch.
> —Matches wrapped in foil and dropped inside
> the locked tin box.
> —Shutters up.
> —Lightbulbs out.

—Master powerswitch turned off.
—Door lifted shut.
—Latch closed.
—Screen door locked and nail at the top left
   corner.
—Keys in hand.
—Wind restored.
—Cottage closed.

§

Then he walks with me to the water.

I hate leaving the cottage. My throat is tight, so I don't speak. He is no longer a stranger. This becomes difficult. Things count now. I wait.

He stoops, picks up a dull sandstone chip and puts it in my hand. "We'll put it back exactly where we found it when we come back in the spring." He even knows enough to go up and wait inside the car.

He can come back. He has passed the tests. I have not chosen badly. After one more look at the water and the wind-twisted trees at its edge, I manage the walk up to the car.

§

For the first time as duenna, I rise to wipe my eyes with fingers red from clay cranes, and I put the cottage in the rearview mirror until spring.